Cole

Book One in the Ride Series

Megan O'Brien

Print ISBN: 978-0-692-22540-0

Megan
O'Brien
Books

To my readers, thank you for making my dream come true!

Prologue

He watched her from his place across the street, his nostrils flaring with anger. Somehow his girl had forgotten that she belonged to him. Clearly she just needed to be reminded, forcefully if necessary. Her place was by his side, and he'd see to it that she returned there before long. He continued to watch with his heart thudding in his chest as he studied her beautiful red hair that tumbled down her back, and the shy smile that lit up her face as she passed an older couple on the street. Even after all this time she was still the most beautiful girl – now woman – that he'd ever seen. His eyes trailed down her curvaceous body with an insatiable feeling of possession. She was headed to work at the brewery on third. He'd been watching her for weeks and was familiar with her schedule. It wasn't difficult. She pretty much just worked and hung out with that little raven-haired roommate of hers. There was no other man to get in his way, not that that would stop him. She'd been gone over eight years and he'd come to claim what was rightfully his. Her time was almost up – he was done waiting.

Chapter One

"Sorry sweetheart, like I said, the part's not gonna be here until Friday," the bored-looking mechanic told me yet again. He didn't even bother looking up from his computer screen as I tried to keep my anger in check.

"First of all, don't call me sweetheart," I replied impatiently while straightening my shoulders.

That at least earned me some eye contact.

"And second of all, you've had my car for over four days now, two more days longer than we agreed," I pointed out as a drill started up in the distance. "I know for a fact that over three supply shops within twenty miles carry the part you need, so why don't you explain to me why it's taking so goddamn long to fix my car?" I demanded, hearing a low chuckle behind me that I ignored. The mechanic's brows shot up in surprise at my unexpected knowledge.

"What, girls can't do research?" I asked tartly.

"I'll make a call," he mumbled after a moment.

"You do that," I replied, crossing my arms over my chest gesturing that I'd wait while he did it right then.

I might have taken it a little easier on the guy except for the fact that I took the bus to the shop expecting to leave with my car. The thought of another bus ride in the 90-degree weather was far from appealing. Plus, getting around without my wheels was a serious pain in the ass. I narrowed my eyes and tapped my toe as the mechanic stared at my chest instead of picking up the phone. Nope, on second thought, wouldn't have taken it easier on him regardless of the heat. He mumbled something incoherent before finally picking the phone up to dial.

"Shit, sure as hell wouldn't want to get on your bad side," a voice muttered, while a low chuckle sounded again behind me.

I turned around to see who was so amused with my situation only to feel my heart stop and then restart inside my chest. He was tall, well over six feet with dirty blond, unruly hair and the brightest blue eyes I'd ever seen. His lips were full and were currently quirked into an amused sexy-as-all-hell smile. His tight, black T-shirt clung to his muscular chest and slim waist in a way that made my mouth dry. He screamed confidence and testosterone right down to his motorcycle boots –something I was far too familiar with from my youth. Of course he had to be a biker, the one type of guy I'd sworn off for life and had done everything in my power to distance myself from. His blue eyes looked intensely down into mine in a way that felt much too intimate, and I steeled myself against the butterflies in my stomach.

"Yeah, well you try being without a car for the better part of a week and see how it affects your mood," I replied coolly.

"Fair enough," he grinned. "Though I'd go easy on poor Manny, I think you're making him nervous," he whispered while leaning toward me. I could almost feel the heat coming off of him and I chastised myself for having such a physical reaction to a complete stranger.

I rolled my eyes, forcing myself not to return his smile. I was sure that smile got him whatever he wanted the majority of the time, and I was far too practiced with his type to let it phase me.

I heard Manny hang up the phone and I turned back to him expectantly.

"Okay, I can get the part before the end of the day and your car will be ready tomorrow," he told me gruffly.

"It's a miracle," I grumbled sarcastically.

He huffed, clearly irritated, all while continuing to allow his eyes to wander below eye level.

I rolled my eyes. "Fine, I'll be back tomorrow to pick it up," I sighed, not at all excited about hoofing it back to the bus stop instead of being able to drive off in my car.

"Sorry for the hassle," he threw in half-heartedly.

"Yeah, you seem real torn up," I snorted, throwing my purse over my shoulder. I forced myself not to spare another glance at the gorgeous man behind me, and I strode out into the hot sun.

I could feel his eyes boring holes into my back. I had to admit that I was pleased as all hell that I'd worn my cute jean shorts that showed off my toned legs, cowboy boots, and a form fitting tank top that displayed just a hint of cleavage. I'd always been well endowed, but when I was younger, my chest had made me self-conscious. As I'd gotten older, I'd become more confident about my body. I didn't try to cover up, but I didn't flaunt my assets either. I tossed my long, slightly wild hair over my shoulder and took a deep breath before facing the inevitable and crossing the street toward my stop.

"Wait up a second," I heard the biker's deep voice call behind me in a commanding tone. I turned to face him, surprised to see him following me.

"I'll give you a ride," he informed me, his blue eyes covered by a pair of wayfarers. He looked down at me as a small smile quirked at the edges of his beautiful mouth.

I looked at him in surprise before shaking my head. "Thanks, but no. I'll catch the bus," I declined.

He tilted his head to the side, seeming to study me for a moment. "It's going to take you twice as long to take the bus and I can tell you're not thrilled at the prospect." He was grinning now, clearly enjoying himself.

"Who would be?" I replied. Despite the warnings in my head I couldn't help but let out a short laugh at his teasing grin. "But I don't know you, and I wouldn't be comfortable getting in a car with you or having you know where I live," I bluntly stated.

"What if it's on a bike and you tell me to drop you a few blocks from home?" he bargained with a slow smile.

I inwardly groaned. Of course it was a bike. And, the truth was that my resolve was wavering. I was beginning to sweat just standing there and the thought of my journey home taking ten minutes as opposed to an hour sounded pretty enticing.

"It's only a ride I swear," he said earnestly, taking his sunglasses off so I could see his eyes. It was a gesture that I found to be surprisingly thoughtful. "And all these guys are witness to you leaving with me," he grinned, pointing to the bustling mechanic shop.

"Yeah, because they're all such upstanding citizens," I muttered, making him laugh.

He got a sudden twinkle in his eye and pulled out his

phone. He dialed and held it to his ear all while smiling down at me.

"Hank? Yeah, is Ettie around?" he asked while I stared at him in confusion. "I just need her to do me a quick favor," he explained. "Etts? Hey, I'm standin' here outside Manny's garage trying to convince this absolutely gorgeous girl to let me give her a ride home."

My mouth opened in shock as he winked at me.

"But she seems to think that she might not be one hundred percent safe with me. I was hoping that woman to woman, you might be able to vouch for me." He listened for a moment and chuckled, the attractive sound shooting right through to my already galloping heart. "Yeah? Ok, thanks," he said as he handed the phone over to me. "Name's Cole by the way, phone's for you." He winked again. I didn't know whether to be annoyed or thoroughly charmed.

I took the phone and held it to my ear. "Hello?" I asked cautiously.

"Hi, this is Ettie. Who's this?" a friendly sounding female voice chirped from the other end.

"Scarlet," I replied, watching Cole's reaction to hearing my name. His eyebrows rose and I thought I detected pleasure in his expression.

"Well Scarlet, I know we've never met, but I've known Cole for over five years. He and my old man are good friends," she explained while I looked everywhere but at the gorgeous blue eyes twinkling down at me. "You couldn't be safer than with him," she continued. "He's a really safe driver and I swear he's not a serial killer," she said as she giggled. "He must really like you if he's so determined to give you a ride," she mused.

"Um, ok thanks," I replied, cutting her off. I didn't want to think too hard as to why he wanted so badly to give me a ride home.

"Have fun!" she said, and then laughed before hanging up.

I handed the phone to him and he took it back looking as though he was going to continue to dial.

"What are you doing?" I asked in confusion.

"Continuing my reference check," he replied, completely serious.

I couldn't help it, I let out a deep belly laugh. I couldn't remember the last time I'd laughed so freely with a complete stranger, but it felt good. There was something about him that I trusted despite all my best efforts not to. "It's okay. I think one reference is sufficient, along with our esteemed witnesses over there," I replied, gesturing back to the mechanic shop.

"Glad to hear it," he grinned.

I followed him back to his gorgeous Harley. Despite my aversion to bikers, I loved bikes and it had been far too long since I'd been on the back of one.

"Have you ridden a bike before?" he asked, throwing on his leather jacket, the patch on the back confirming what I'd known right away, that he belonged to a motorcycle club.

"A time or two," I admitted, forcing myself to keep a straight face. He eyed me speculatively for a moment while he clasped his helmet beneath his chin. God, he was gorgeous. It was so unfair.

He handed me a spare helmet. The same helmet that I'm sure he gave to every woman who rode on the back of his bike. I threw a leg over the bike, as the engine roared to life, and hopped up behind him. I sighed with the familiarity of it all – it was like being back home.

"Where am I goin'?" he asked loudly over the noise of the bike.

"Do you know where the high school is?" I asked.

He nodded.

"Take a left at the school and I'll guide you from there," I told him.

"Okay, hang on darlin'," he replied with a grin.

I rolled my eyes but obliged by wrapping my arms around his leather clad torso, secretly loving the feel of his body in front of mine as we took off out of the parking lot. I couldn't fight my grin as we roared through town. I absolutely loved every second of the ride, and having my arms around such a gorgeous guy wasn't half bad either. My inner thighs rested snugly against him, and I had to force my mind off of the tingles that shot through me from the intimate contact. I was surprised that I felt safe enough to direct him to my apartment instead of to a few houses down. I was enjoying the ride so much that it felt like we were pulling up to the curb in what felt like seconds. He turned off the bike as I swung off and unfastened the helmet.

"Thanks for the ride," I said sincerely, raking my fingers through my now very tousled hair.

He watched my fingers for a moment before meeting my eyes. "You're welcome," he replied, accepting the helmet I handed back to him.

"How about you give me your number and we can go for a ride again sometime?" he offered with a smile that was broad enough to show his dimple. Why did he have to be a biker of all things?

"I can't," I replied quietly, meeting his intense gaze.

"Boyfriend?" he asked.

I shook my head. "I um…" I muttered as I struggled with how to respond without sounding like a total bitch. I decided that honesty was the best method. "I don't date bikers," I said with a shrug.

His brows rose in amused surprise. "You don't date bikers?" he repeated. "I've never seen a girl enjoy being on the back of a bike more, but you don't date bikers," he said as he chuckled.

I could feel the blush creep over my cheeks. "That sounds about right," I admitted. "Thanks again for the ride, it was nice to meet you," I replied quickly before I did something really stupid like agree to see him again.

"Don't you want to know my last name?" he called as I turned toward my place.

"Nope," I called back over my shoulder.

I could hear his chuckle over the roar of the engine as he started up the bike. I let myself into my apartment with shaking hands and forced myself not to give him one last glance before he rode off.

"Was that a Harley I heard?" my roommate and best friend, Kat, asked incredulously when I shut the door behind me and leaned against it heavily.

"Yep," I muttered.

"Oh, this I have to hear," she said with grin.

Kat and I had known each other since I'd moved to Nevada eight years ago. She was the only person who knew absolutely everything about me, including why I had an aversion to bikers. Unfortunately my aversion didn't mean that I wasn't attracted to them – things would be a hell of a lot easier if it did.

"I need a beer," I grumbled, dropping my purse and heading toward the fridge.

Our place was simple but well maintained. Despite the somewhat shady neighborhood, our landlord took pride in the building. Our apartment was on the second floor and faced the street, which wasn't great for security, but I'd never felt unsafe. It had an open living room with hardwood floors. The whole place had high ceilings and felt airy and open, which helped during the summer when we stayed inside a lot because of the heat. The kitchen was a simple galley style with dated appliances that by some miracle continued to work. One of my favorite parts of the kitchen was the bar that we'd furnished with four stools. Instead of using a dining table and chairs, we ate there. Neither one of us cooked a lot or entertained much at our place so we didn't need anything fancy. Both of us had good-sized bedrooms, and we had a small stone-covered patio that was just big enough for the grill we never used.

Our living situation had always worked perfectly for us. Kat preferred to go out and I preferred to be at home. But other than our social preferences, we spent the majority of our time together. We even worked together, both as waitresses at the brewery downtown. Ever since Kat had forced her way into my life with her spitfire-like nature, we never looked back. We had lived together in various places ever since.

When I left California I'd meant to get farther from home, much farther. But I'd run out of money, and by the time I had enough to get back on the road I was reluctant to leave Kat. She was my partner in crime and the best friend I'd ever had. So, I stayed with just one state line between me and my past life.

I sat heavily on the couch, thankful to be out of the heat of the day, and told her about my biker run in.

"Damn, I wish I would have peeked through the blinds!" she exclaimed when I was done.

I laughed and nodded. "I'm not talking him up, he was that hot," I sighed.

"Damn, too bad," she muttered. "Well, you can catch a ride with me tonight – we're working the same shift," she said, patting my leg while getting up. Kat always knew when to change the subject. It was one of the endless things I loved about her.

"Cool, thanks," I said.

"And, because I'm such an awesome best friend, I'll drive you to get your car tomorrow, too," Kat said with a grin.

"You're the best."

We worked the late shift, and though I had more than enough distraction, my mind kept drifting back to Cole. I hurried from table to table taking orders and serving drinks, but my mind was miles away. No man had ever incited such a physical reaction from me. I found it both off-putting and electrifying – two emotions I wasn't accustomed to feeling at the same time. With the latter rarely being felt at all.

"Earth to Scar, are you in there?" Kat teased as we were driving home, both exhausted and smelling like burgers and beer. It was one of the pitfalls of the job.

"Shut up," I grumbled before throwing her a small smile.

"You've got biker on the brain," she said as she giggled.

"Do not," I grumbled.

"Do too, liar." She laughed before letting the subject

drop.

I dragged my tired, lying ass to bed and tried in vain not to think about that damned dimpled grin.

Thankfully, my car was ready when Kat drove me to pick it up the following day. My Pathfinder was nothing fancy, but it was practical and it was all mine, which always meant something to me. I was extremely happy to have it back.

"Here, I'm supposed to give you this," Manny grumbled when I paid my bill. He handed me over an envelope and I looked at him in confusion.

"Don't look at me," he said as he shrugged, turning back to his paperwork. I walked over to my car while reading the note that I took out of the envelope. I was soon grinning despite myself.

"The last name's Jackson, just in case you wanted to do a background check. Here's my number: 540-8970. Use it."

I couldn't help but grin at his flippancy. I folded up the note and put it in my purse, flattered that he'd taken the time to come back to the shop to leave it for me. Clearly, this was a man who was used to getting what he wanted. Unfortunately for him, in this instance, he was in for a rude awakening.

Chapter Two

"Scar, come on, seriously. You never go out," Kat whined a week later trying her best for the hundredth time to get me to accompany her to our coworker's birthday party. I rolled my eyes at her and turned my attention back to my movie. "Ok, you know what? Consider this an intervention," she said firmly, snapping the TV off and standing in front of it with her hands on her hips.

"Hey!" I protested.

"No, seriously Scarlet. This is ridiculous. All you do is work, read, and work out. You're heartbreakingly gorgeous, you're young, and you need to live," she said forcefully. "I'm not saying you need to come out just to meet some guy, but come out just to be out," she insisted. "It'll be fun, remember fun?" she pressed.

I sighed, reluctant to admit that she was right. I knew I probably guarded myself too closely, that I should get out more. The only socializing I really did was when we had people over, or when we had drinks with coworkers at the bar after our shifts. But I liked feeling in control and safe, something that could only be attained by keeping my world relatively small. It had felt big and harsh enough for the first eighteen years.

"Please?" she pleaded one last time.

"Fine," I replied, and surprised us both.

"Really? Ok, great!" she exclaimed, jumping up and down. "This will be so much fun!"

Kat was clearly enjoying getting ready together. I felt somewhat reluctant. I'd guarded myself so closely for the last eight years. I hadn't changed my name or anything as extreme as that, but I'd tried hard to stay under the radar. Rationally, every time she successfully dragged me out, I knew that one night out wouldn't change anything, but it made me feel oddly vulnerable. I forced myself to shake it off and to enjoy a night out with my best friend.

Kat decided on skinny jeans and a figure hugging tank top that complemented her slender frame. She kept her eye makeup relatively simple, but chose bright red lipstick that offset her raven hair, which was cut short for the summer. She had beautiful blue eyes that complemented her dark hair and pale, porcelain skin. She was a complete and total knockout.

My figure was much curvier than hers, with my large breasts and an ass that only frequent exercise could tame. I was tall for a girl and I worked out often, so I always looked slender, but I was no stick figure that was for sure. I chose a lightweight summer dress that hugged my hips and showed some leg. It had a modest neckline with an open back, which made it sexier than the average summer dress. I paired it with my platform sandals and left my long hair down and naturally wavy. I did a smoky eye, which made my green, almond-shaped eyes pop, but I went with a nude lip gloss so I didn't look too overdone. All in all, I thought we both looked pretty fantastic.

We hopped in a cab and were soon headed downtown to our coworker's birthday party at some bar I'd unsurprisingly never heard of. The place was packed when we arrived, and Kat automatically took my hand and pulled me toward the bar to order drinks.

I was pleased to find that it wasn't even an hour into the party and I was having fun. The music was good and several of our other coworkers were there. Everyone was so excited that I showed up. It made me realize how much I needed to get out more. Connie, the birthday girl, had greeted us enthusiastically. Connie was upbeat and always seemed to be in a good mood. I often thought that I should have some of whatever she was having to make her so seemingly high on life. She soon introduced me to her boyfriend, Wes, whom I had seen in the brewery a few times but hadn't met formally. They were an interesting match. Connie looked like your typical California girl with her blond hair and tanned skin, while Wes was dark skinned and somewhat menacing with his large frame and shaved head.

Wes seemed nice enough, though he was clearly guarded. He watched Connie with a kind of intensity that I envied. He obviously cared deeply for her and was protective in a way that I found to be sweet instead of suffocating. I hadn't thought about my own love life in so long, and I suddenly realized that I was lonely. Aside from a casual date here and there, I hadn't had a serious boyfriend since I'd left home. I missed the intimacy of it, the comfort. I was shocked and even a bit disgusted that I could think back to my time with Jake with any type of yearning given the way things had ended.

My thoughts shifted to Cole as they had often done

in the past week, and I thought of the note I'd kept in my purse. I hadn't thrown it out despite considering it often. I had to admit that I'd had more than one fantasy about him since we met. I shook my head to dispel the current direction of my thoughts, and I excused myself from the table to go get another drink.

"Can I buy you a drink?" a guy said with a smile as I walked up to the bar. He was far too preppy for my taste, but handsome in his own way. He also looked like he'd had one too many drinks.

"No thanks," I said as I shook my head politely.

"Just one drink," he pleaded, trying to lay the charm on, but immediately turned me off in the process. "You're the most beautiful girl in the room," he murmured, his hand drifting to my bare back. I stepped back immediately, planning to head back to my friends, but his hand clamped firmly on my arm. "Hey, where are you goin'?" he asked, his eyes traveling down my figure.

"If you want to keep that hand, you better remove it in two fucking seconds," a voice growled angrily behind me. My heart leapt at the familiarity of it, and I inwardly scolded myself for the involuntary flutter that fled through my entire body. What was he doing here? How long had he been standing there?

The guy at the bar looked slightly taken aback, but he quickly removed his hand. "Sorry, just a bit of harmless fun," he explained casually.

I narrowed my eyes at him before turning to face the formidable frame of Cole, who was still glaring angrily at preppy guy.

"What are you doing?" I asked nervously. I was completely befuddled at seeing him.

Instead of answering, he shocked me by putting an arm around me and leading me toward the other end of the bar as though he'd done it a thousand times. I couldn't pretend that I didn't enjoy that short walk pressed against his firm body. And I may have leaned in to take a sniff of him, just a small one. He smelled amazing, of course.

"Newcastle," he ordered from the bartender who'd come over within moments of seeing Cole standing there. I carefully edged out from under his arm, despite wanting very much to stay right there.

"And for you?" the bartender asked me. Cole looked down at me expectantly. He still looked angry and I thought it best not to argue with him.

"Gin and tonic please," I requested. I let Cole pay for my drink, still too flabbergasted to argue.

"I assume you got my note," his deep voice rumbled before taking a deep swallow of his beer. God, his mouth was beautiful.

I nodded.

He looked at me expectantly, his eyes fierce.

"It's not personal," I assured him, feeling flustered by his nearness and his intense stare. The man did not mince words, that was for sure. He looked gorgeous in dark blue jeans and a dark blue Henley that made his eyes pop. Tattoos ran up and down both arms, complementing the muscle that flexed as he moved. He searched my expression in that way of his that made me feel like he could see right through me, and I was forced to look away.

"Where's the rest of your dress?" he demanded, the change in the conversation throwing me for a loop.

"Excuse me?" I demanded in return, any trace of feeling flustered disappearing.

"You heard me," he replied as we stared at each other, the electricity zapping between us.

"Thanks for the drink. Goodnight, Cole," I bit out, and turned on my heel to stomp away. I didn't get one foot before his hand gripped my arm and spun me around to face him.

"Didn't say you don't look hotter than hell baby, but it's gonna make for an exhausting night for me if I have to wade in every time some mother fucker looks at you the wrong way," he informed me.

I stared at him in utter bafflement for a minute before I collected myself. Seriously the nerve of this guy!

"I'm sorry, I must have missed something," I said sarcastically. "The last I checked, I was perfectly capable of taking care of myself. There's no position currently open for 'Scarlet's savior,'" I said as I put my hand to my chest dramatically. "The whole damsel in distress thing isn't really my bag, so clearly you've got the wrong girl," I added, as I took a sip of my drink and forced myself not to look away from his now thunderous expression.

"Scar! There you are," Kat's voice sounded from behind me. She stopped short after observing my stare down with Cole, the energy still crackling between us. I turned to her, grateful for the distraction. Her expression was almost comical as she took Cole in, her mouth practically agape.

"Cole, this is Kat," I introduced begrudgingly. "My best friend and roommate," I added.

"Nice to meet you," he replied, shaking her hand, barely sparing her a glance before his eyes returned to mine.

She grinned and I knew she'd made the connection of who he was. She'd be gloating later that she had forced me to come out tonight. "Do you want to join us?" she offered. I narrowed my eyes at her. She was so in for it.

"Love to," he smirked with a devilish gleam in his eye. Clearly his mood had lifted while mine was still far from light. I rolled my eyes as he followed us back to the table. Wes and his buddies all turned to greet Cole with clear familiarity.

I narrowed my eyes at him again as he laughed and said, "It's a small world, sweetheart."

"You know Wes and Connie?" I asked, surprised.

"Wes and I go way back. That's why I'm here tonight, to hang with him," he said. "Not filling any job openings tonight," he added in my ear with a grin. His proximity sent a thrill through me, which served to only sour my mood. I was determined not to fall for this guy's routine. And, it was just that, a routine – one I was sure he'd done a thousand times. Once he'd overcome the challenge I presented, I would be history, and I had no interest in being a part of that.

"Hmph," I muttered. I sat back in my old seat with Kat and Connie on my right, and he took a place at my left where he leaned over to talk to his friends in that deep voice of his. Kat nudged me from the side and I could tell she was grinning from ear to ear without even looking at her.

"He's freaking hot, Scar," she whispered a bit too loudly in my ear. She'd had a few too many cocktails.

I refused to respond to her, all too aware that Cole's conversation had ended and he was probably listening. He threw his arm over the chair I sat in, and I realized he was staking a claim in typical biker fashion. Much to my dismay, I found myself a bit turned on by the gesture. There was no denying the sexual energy that passed between us no matter how hard I tried to ignore it. I needed to get away from him soon before I ended up doing something I really regretted, like tackling him. The man infuriated me, but I had never been so attracted to someone in my life. Just the press of his outer thigh against mine underneath the table was making it hard for me to concentrate.

He didn't force small talk on me, but instead kept close to me as we each talked with our friends. Connie and I kept ourselves entertained by trying to find suitable guys for Kat, but the pickings were somewhat limited.

"What are you girls giggling about so much over there?" Cole's deep voice rumbled next to my ear, making my heart gallop in my chest.

"Trying to find a guy for Kat," I answered honestly. "So far, not much to choose from," I added while drinking the dredges of my cocktail.

"Need another?" he asked, eyeing my empty glass.

"I can get it," I replied firmly.

"You can say whatever you like about it, but I think my limit for keeping assholes at bay has already been met for the evening, darlin'. And with you in that dress, you walk up to the bar and I'm sure that preppy asshole won't be alone. So how about you let me get it and save us both the hassle?" he persuaded, his arm still wrapped around my chair as his fingers began tracing my shoulder in a way that made me want to scream... and not with fear.

"Listen, I appreciate the... whatever you're trying to do," I sighed with a wave of my hand.

His brows rose in amusement as he watched me, his face mere inches from mine.

"But your efforts are lost on me. You should find some

other girl whose going to go home with you, because I'm not," I said firmly, gesturing around the room to all of the potential one-night stands at his fingertips.

"Are you always this much of a pain in the ass?" he demanded, his eyes incredulous.

"Just trying to save you some time," I replied.

"Another gin and tonic?" he asked as though I hadn't spoken.

"Suit yourself," I shrugged, before nodding that he had my drink right. He squeezed the back of my neck briefly before he stood up to head to the bar. The gesture stoked the fire I already had simmering for him. It was possessive and yet reassuring. I liked it a lot. I tried not to watch his ass as he walked away, but those Levis fit him entirely too well for me not to.

"How do you know Cole?" Connie asked excitedly, taking the opportunity to get the scoop, and forcing me to swallow the saliva in my mouth and tear my eyes from his ass.

I shrugged, a bit embarrassed that I'd been caught ogling him. "I don't really, he was at my mechanic shop last week and he ended up giving me a ride home. Now he's here." I shrugged.

"Something tells me he intends to get to know you a lot better," she replied.

I wrinkled my nose. "I don't date bikers," I uttered quickly.

"Honey, I don't care if he's a freaking alien from outer space. If Cole Jackson takes a shine to you, you go with it. And that's coming from someone who's madly in love with her boyfriend," she said with a grin.

Despite my reservations, I really wanted to know more.

"What's he like?" I couldn't help but ask, my curiosity overwhelming me.

"I don't know him well," she answered truthfully. "Just hung around him a few times at the club and out and about with Wes. But he keeps to himself a lot. He's always been polite to me, but he's clearly not someone you fuck with," she said, telling me something I already knew.

"Yeah, and how many women have you seen him go home with?" I asked dryly, already knowing the answer to that as well.

"A few," she admitted. "But I have yet to see him stake a claim the way he's doing with you tonight," she added.

"Yeah, that's only because I'm not dropping my panties for him just because he throws me a smile," I replied knowingly. "He just likes the chase."

I'd grown up watching men like Cole, beautiful and powerful men who valued their bikes more than the women on their arms. Because of who my father was, they'd stayed clear for the most part, but I'd watched them go through women like water. It had always baffled me how the women hung around the club just hoping for more, ready to be used at a moment's notice. That had never been for me, and being my father's daughter, he would have killed anyone who tried anyway. My father had been overprotective (to say the least), and at times it had driven me crazy. Now I just missed his guidance and protection. I missed everything about him, every day.

Kat snorted, speaking for the first time and snapped me back out of my thoughts. "Or it could be that you're devastatingly gorgeous and smart and he knows he's met his match."

"You're biased," I pointed out dryly, as Cole returned

with my drink ending any further discussion.

"Thanks," I said, as he handed me my drink and reclaimed his seat next to me.

"Don't mention it," he replied easily.

"Anyone try to feel you up?" I teased, taking a sip. As long as he knew where I stood I might as well have a little fun.

He chuckled. "Only one person in here I'd let do that. Anyone else would lose a limb," he replied, looking at me with a twinkle in his eye.

I blushed and turned my attention back to the bar at large, which was now packed beyond anything I'd ever seen.

"Is it always like this?" I found myself asking him.

"What? This busy?"

I nodded.

He shrugged. "I don't come here a lot, I take it you don't either, but I'd say this isn't all that unusual."

I simply nodded, watching the crowd, feeling slightly annoyed with all the people.

"This wouldn't be your choice of venue?" he asked while leaning into me, his arm draped over my chair.

I shook my head. "Actually, I don't go out much," I admitted before immediately wishing I hadn't said that.

"Why's that?"

I pondered his question, unsure how to answer him.

"It's a simple question, sweetheart," he added when I hesitated.

"You can't ask the question and then define what a simple answer is," I replied, feeling slightly affronted.

He shocked me by taking my chin and gently turning my face so I was looking at him. He looked at me with such tenderness that it made my stomach pitch. "Fair enough," he murmured, moving to squeeze the back of my neck again with his large hand. His touch, yet again, sent spikes of pleasure through me.

"This place is way too crowded," Connie complained loudly over the music. "Let's go somewhere else."

This was a perfect opportunity for me to make my escape. If I sat next to Cole any longer, and God forbid, in a more intimate environment, I was done for. There were too many elements from my past that reminded me to stay away from him. "Connie, I think I may actually head home," I told her over the noise as I felt Cole stiffen at my side.

"What! No you can't," she complained. "It's too much fun getting to hang out with you, for once," she emphasized with a raised brow.

"How about I promise to come out more often?" I bargained with a smile.

She pouted for a moment before shrugging. "Fine. But I'm holding you to that," she warned before hugging me good-bye.

Kat turned to me and we exchanged a look. She was gauging her chances of convincing me to stay, and I was silently telling her that it wasn't going to happen. She nodded simply and sighed.

"See you at home," I said.

"Thanks again for the drink. And for defending my honor, warranted or not," I said to Cole, and smiled slightly as I gathered my purse.

"You can thank me when I've dropped you off in front of your place," his voice rumbled.

I looked up at him with wide eyes. "What? No, I'm just

calling a cab. You stay and hang out with your friends," I argued, my anxiety rising as I realized that he wasn't going to go away as easily as I'd hoped.

Instead of answering me, he turned to his friends and started issuing farewells. There were many handshakes and rough man hugs before he turned to me expectantly, gesturing that I could lead the way. Great, now I had no way of getting out of this, and everyone would now think we were going home together. I groaned under my breath, but I started to make my way through the crowd, waving to Connie and Kat who looked beyond thrilled about the situation. I rolled my eyes at them. I felt a warm, large hand press on my bare back, guiding me protectively through the masses of drunken people.

"Are you okay to drive?" I asked, thinking about it for the first time as we got out into the fresh air and much quieter street.

"Wouldn't offer to drive you if I wasn't," he answered simply, shrugging on his leather jacket.

"Okay," I murmured as I followed him to his bike.

"You don't have a jacket?" he asked reproachfully.

"Ending the night on a Harley Sportster wasn't really part of my plan," I answered dryly.

He looked at me for a moment before shrugging. "Fair enough," he said, and he smiled as he handed me his spare helmet. "You know your Harleys, huh?" he asked as I climbed up behind him carefully, trying to keep my dress in place.

"You could say that," I muttered simply.

He gave me a look as though he wanted to pry, but thought better of it and instead started the bike up.

We roared off toward my house and I had to admit

that, yet again, I loved being on his bike. It felt exhilarating yet safe – dual emotions seemed to be commonplace in his company.

When we pulled up to my building, I immediately stiffened and sucked in my breath. Our front door was slightly ajar, certainly not the way we'd left it.

Cole turned off the bike as I stayed glued to the seat, fear percolating through my system.

When I hadn't moved he shifted slightly to look at me. "What is it?" he asked, his eyes following my widened gaze.

"Our door... it's open," I breathed, pointing to our front door.

"What the fuck?" he rumbled, swinging off the bike and stalking toward the building before I could stop him. "Stay there," he ordered over his shoulder. Not something he had to tell me twice. My mind whirled with the possibilities. Was it just a random break in or something more? All of a sudden the gin and tonics weren't sitting so well in my stomach as I wondered if my past had suddenly become my present. I hadn't seen or heard from anyone in my old life since I'd left, but I'd always watched my back in fear that my past would come looming up to haunt me.

It felt like hours, but it was probably only minutes before Cole was walking back toward the bike.

"Whoever got in there is gone now," he confirmed once he reached me, and I climbed off the bike feeling slightly shaky on my feet. "Granted, I haven't seen your place before, but everything looks orderly," he added.

I simply nodded, looking over at my door.

"You gonna call the cops?" he asked.

I thought about that for a second before I shook my head. I tried to fly under the radar, so I didn't need a police report circulating. Someone from Dad's old crew might get wind of it, get worried, and decide it was time to check in despite my making it clear when I left that such a visit would not be welcomed.

"Thank you for driving me home and for checking things out," I said quietly while taking the helmet off. "I'll handle it from here," I told him, trying my best to sound confident when I felt anything but.

"Darlin', you would force a saint to lose patience, get back on the bike," he insisted.

"What? And go home with you? No way," I demanded as I shook my head.

"It's either that or I'm coming in there with you," he answered simply with a chin lift toward my place. We regarded each other for a few moments before he softened his approach. "Look, it's true I want in there," he said, his eyes assessing me provocatively as my eyes widened in turn. "You got something that I want a lot more of. But even if I didn't, I sure as fuck wouldn't let you walk in there by yourself and spend the night alone. I promise to keep my hands to myself, alright?" he asked. I was still stuck on his "wanting in there" comment, and it took me a minute to pull myself together. "Alright?" he asked again.

"Okay," I answered him, softly climbing back on the bike. The truth was, I couldn't fathom walking into that dark apartment by myself and being able to sleep a wink, so I decided to put my arms around Cole instead. It wasn't a hard decision when it came down to it.

It was a short drive before we pulled up to a simple, single story house just on the outskirts of town. We pulled into the garage next to what I assumed was his black F-150 truck. Clearly he did well for himself.

Despite my current frazzled state, I took a minute to look around. We'd walked in through the garage straight into a large, open kitchen with wood counter tops and a beautiful island that looked like it had been custom made. His appliances were stainless steel, but nothing too flashy. The kitchen opened up to a large living room with hardwood floors and high beamed ceilings. It was furnished relatively simply with black leather couches, a coffee table, and a huge TV and entertainment system. A hallway to the left looked like it led to the rest of the house.

"I have to call Kat," I told him as soon as I'd put my purse down on his sofa.

He nodded while heading off to the fridge, and I soon found myself holding a cold, much welcomed beer as I let the phone ring. She didn't answer, which didn't surprise me, so I left her a message and followed it with a text letting her know briefly what happened and that she should sleep elsewhere tonight. I felt immediate guilt, hoping like hell it wasn't me who caused this situation and that it was just random bad luck.

Cole flopped down next to me on the couch and crossed his legs at the ankle on the coffee table and flipped on the TV. I suddenly wished I was wearing more clothing and shivered slightly in the forced air of his place.

"Cold?" he asked quietly.

I nodded and he got up and handed me a Harley Davidson hoodie that I gratefully put on over my dress. It was huge on me, but it made me feel moderately more at ease.

"Thanks," I sighed, sitting back on the couch and propping my now bare feet on the edge of his table. He put an arm around me and pulled me into his side, surprising me.

"Just relax," his voice rumbled when I protested slightly. I had to admit it was comforting to be close to him, and breathing in the smell of him wasn't half bad either. So I allowed myself to sink further into him and zoned out on the mindless home improvement show he'd put on.

Before I knew it, I was being gently lifted and carried. "Hmm?" I muttered.

"Just putting you to bed sleepy girl," his low voice answered me. I didn't have the energy to protest or to wonder where I was sleeping. The night's events had completely worn me out. The last thing I knew, I was being tucked into a warm, soft bed and I fell into oblivion.

Chapter Three

I woke up entirely too hot. It took me several moments to place where I was as my eyes adjusted to the weak light streaming in through the blinds. There was a warm wall of man tucked behind me with a strong arm around my belly. All of last night's craziness and the fact that I was in Cole's bed came rushing back. It had been a long time since I'd been held, especially while I slept, and I allowed myself a few moments to appreciate it before I shifted.

He muttered something in his sleep, but he let me slip out from under his arm so I could take the sweatshirt off that I'd fallen asleep in. I lay back down on my back without touching him and took in the high-beamed ceilings of his bedroom and the simple bed, nightstand, and dresser that made up the room. I looked over at the man beside me and tried not to audibly suck in my breath. He was shirtless with a muscled arm now thrown above his head. His body was more beautiful than I'd imagined, with tanned skin, firm pecks, and a six pack. My eyes turned to the inviting trail of hair that began past his belly button and led to places I couldn't allow myself to contemplate. A large tattoo spanned across his chest, some type of MC insignia. It was the profile of the head of a medieval knight wearing armor. The knight was black and white with red flames that burst out from behind it. I'd always loved tattoos and this one was particularly unique. I forced my eyes away before I did something mortifying like lick him. His bed was comfortable and I realized I'd slept fairly well considering I'd slept in my clothes. I carefully slipped from the bed to use the restroom. I brushed my teeth with my finger before heading out to the kitchen. The least I could do was make him breakfast to thank him.

He emerged not long after, looking gloriously groggy with tousled hair and sleepy blue eyes.

"Hi," he said, while giving me a panty-dropping smile as I turned the bacon on the stove.

"Hi," I said and smiled back. "Coffee?"

"Please," he yawned as I poured him a cup.

"You didn't have to make breakfast," he told me, accepting the cup I offered him and drinking it black as I suspected he would. He leaned against the counter, still shirtless, watching me.

I shrugged, "I don't mind. You have a surprisingly well stocked fridge for a bachelor," I commented with a teasing grin as I flipped the pancakes I'd whipped up. I needed something to keep me from staring openly at his gorgeous torso. He really needed to put on a shirt.

He chuckled. "I like to eat," he said, mischief in his eyes.

"Ah, I knew there had to be a reason." I smiled wryly and put a heaping plate of pancakes and bacon in front of him as he sat down at the bar.

"Aren't you going to eat?" he asked after swallowing his first, very large bite.

I shook my head and wrinkled my nose. "Not too

hungry this morning. But I don't typically eat a big breakfast anyway," I said, sipping my coffee and turning to clean up the mess I'd made.

"Did you hear back from Kat?" he asked.

I nodded. "She texted me, she's fine. We'll meet back up at our place later and go from there," I told him.

"How'd you two meet?" he asked. "You seem really close," he observed accurately.

I smiled and nodded in agreement. "We met at a coffee shop. She worked there at the time. I would go in every morning and she was so damned friendly."

He laughed at my expression.

"And we just became friends," I said with a shrug. I left out the part where I was going into the coffee shop because I had nowhere else to go, and I was desperate to get out of the flea bag motel I was staying in. I started working at the coffee shop along with her soon after we met.

"You workin' today?" he asked.

I nodded. "Not till later though," I said as I remembered that I told him briefly last night that I waited tables at Jupiter.

"How about you?" I asked carefully. We had yet to delve into his line of work.

He shrugged. "I make my own hours, one of the benefits of being in the family business," he explained. I fought the urge to roll my eyes. I knew the aspects of "family business" all too well.

Not wanting to know more, I ignored his vague response and finished cleaning.

"Thanks, that was delicious," he said, patting his firm stomach. "I can't remember the last time someone cooked me breakfast."

My inner cynic rolled her eyes. I was pretty certain that Cole had his fair share of bedmates and I'd be surprised if one or two of them didn't try to charm him with breakfast now and then.

I felt mildly depressed at the thought. "Do you mind taking me home now?" I asked quietly.

He eyed me thoughtfully for a few moments before he nodded. "Let me just throw on some clothes."

He emerged shortly after bearing the same hoodie I'd worn the night before. "You'll probably be more comfortable wearing this on the bike," he explained.

"Thanks," I said, appreciating the thought.

"I just have to swing by to give something to my Pop and then I'll take you home," he surprised me by saying.

I had no choice but to agree, I was pretty much at his mercy and he'd already done a lot for me. But meeting his father wasn't high on my list of things I wanted to do, especially when I was trying desperately to keep my distance from him.

We were soon pulling up to what I assumed was the MC clubhouse. I was shocked that he would bring me here. Typically, only old ladies hung around the club, or loose women who slept with the bikers. I was neither, but I tried not to think much of it. I hadn't been inside a club since I'd left my father's eight years ago when I turned eighteen.

"This'll be quick," he assured me as he led me into the front room that smelled like leather, beer, and men. It took my eyes a moment to adjust to the dim light of the expansive room where every shade was drawn, most likely to keep the heat out. Despite that effort, it was warm, and I wished I could take the sweatshirt off that covered a large amount of my body. My eyes continued to span the room.

finding a fully stocked bar in the right corner and a pool table sitting in the middle. There appeared to be offices off to the left and I knew from experience that only seasoned club members would occupy one of those. The floor was dark hardwood that squeaked underfoot. The feel of the place along with its décor reminded me swiftly and reverently of home. I was shocked when a lump formed in my throat that I desperately forced down. I missed my father every day, and this place reminded me so fiercely of him, it felt like he was about to walk through the door.

"Cole, that you?" a gruff voice hollered from an office to the right.

"Yeah, Pop," Cole called back.

An older man emerged who bore a striking resemblance to Cole. His hair was grayer and he had the telltale lines of age surrounding his face, but his eyes were the same bright blue. His graying hair was held back in a long ponytail. He had a mustache and a goatee that suited his handsome face.

"Who's this?" he asked, gesturing to me with a lift of his chin.

"This is Scarlet. I'm giving her a ride home, but it sounded like this couldn't wait," Cole replied somewhat impatiently. "Scarlet, this is my Pop, Cal Jackson," he introduced. Something about the name was familiar but I ignored it and waved shyly feeling ridiculous wearing Cole's giant sweatshirt and undoubtedly looking like some floosy he'd brought home the night before.

"Nice to meet you," I said. Cal eyed me for several moments. It seemed like he was trying to place me, but then he snapped out of it. "You, too. We won't be but a minute," he responded, leading Cole toward the back and leaving me standing alone in the room.

I took a deep breath, trying to push down the strong emotions this place was bringing out in me. I wandered to the wood paneled walls and looked at the various photos framed throughout the room. Many of them boasted pictures of Cal when he was younger, and I immediately surmised that he was the MC President. There were a few of younger children, a beautiful boy I picked out immediately as Cole when he was around five-years-old. They were all similar to the photos I'd grown up around.

I was still browsing the walls when my eyes stopped and opened wide on a photo of Cal with a wide grin and his arm draped around none other than my father. I sucked in an audible breath and swallowed hard. It must have been taken at least ten years ago, if not longer, and my eyes filled with involuntary tears at seeing the warm smile on my father's face. My fingers drifted to the frame as I tried desperately to get a handle on my emotions. Both men wore their respective club patches proudly on their jackets as they grinned at the camera. The "Sinners" club patch adorned on my father's jacket was one of the most familiar images from my youth. My father loved that club and he raised me to love it, too. It was the only family I'd ever known. The club believed in community and brotherhood, until all that changed.

"You're Ray Malone's girl aren't you?" Cal's gruff voice asked from behind me, sending me whirling around in shock. I hadn't even heard him come in.

I couldn't seem to get any words around the lump in my throat as Cole came up behind his father and eyed my tearful expression with surprise.

"I'd know those green eyes anywhere," Cal continued,

smiling fondly as I stood rooted to the spot unable to speak. "I met you when you were just a little thing, I'm sure you don't remember. Your daddy was so proud of you. Called you his Scarlet Rose," he remembered fondly, sending the tears that filled my eyes spilling down over my cheeks. I wiped them away as quickly as I could.

"How did you know him?" I finally managed.

"Our clubs supported each other from across state lines. Whenever we had business in California we'd stay at your dad's club and vice versa," he explained.

It wasn't uncommon for clubs to be aligned from such a distance, but it explained why Cal wasn't immediately familiar. I'd probably met him very few times during my childhood.

"Over the years we became like family, your father and I. We were a lot alike. Both single fathers. You and Cole played together once or twice when you were little," he explained, and I looked over at Cole whose surprised expression matched mine.

"Never thought the world could be quite this small," I muttered.

"Damn shame about your daddy, honey," he continued. "He was a good man and that club went to shit without him," he muttered angrily.

The circumstances surrounding my father's death were still somewhat of a mystery. He lost control of his bike on his way back from a visit with a neighboring club. He collided with an oncoming car and died on impact. Upon closer inspection, Henry, my father's right hand, had discovered that the brakes had been tampered with. Anyone close to the situation knew that Jake had somehow been involved, but they couldn't prove it.

Jacob and I had grown up together in the club. We'd been best friends since toddlerhood, often driving my parents crazy with our antics. When my mother died of cancer, Jake was a source of unfailing strength for me. He seemed to know just how to get me through those terribly dark days. Years later we became a couple, though I never felt passionately about him. I gave him my virginity and my love, but I was never in love with him.

Then, Jake started to change. He became brooding and removed. His attitude toward me became commanding and aggressive. He was set on having a position of power within the club, but my father didn't like his leadership style, or lack thereof. Jake used force and intimidation to get what he wanted. The men didn't respect him or want to follow him, which served to drive him deeper into anger.

I broke it off with him and I tried my best to stay as far away from him as possible, until he drove me to leave altogether. Even though I had witnessed truly cruel behavior from Jake, and had been a victim of it myself, I still had trouble grappling with the fact that he could have taken my father's life. And though there were times that he had made me fear for my own life, the part of me that remembered him as a dark haired, wide-eyed little boy still couldn't rationalize it.

I stood staring at Cal, a man who could tell me so many stories about my father – someone who could make him feel alive to me through the history they shared. But I couldn't risk the exposure of opening myself up further to him.

"I don't know what your relationship with the Sinners is like now, but I'd appreciate it if you didn't tell anyone that you saw me," I told him, trying to keep any fear out of my tone. I wasn't entirely successful and he didn't miss it.

"You got trouble?" he asked, his eyes sharpening like a hawk's.

Great. I'd gone from flying under the radar to getting the attention of an MC president. "I can take care of myself, but I left home for a reason and I'd like to leave it at that," I requested firmly.

"Your father and I had a code to watch each other's backs. I'll always feel guilt for what happened to him, always wondered if I'd seen the signs that maybe I could have helped. But I sure as hell can keep my end of the bargain when it comes to you. You have the full protection of this club," he said firmly, shocking me. I knew what that meant and it was no small promise or one to be taken lightly. "We're no longer aligned with your dad's club, like I said it went to shit without him and there's some fucked up mother fuckers running it now," he added scornfully.

I couldn't have agreed more. After my father died, Jake and his henchman Victor had somehow clawed their way to the top. I had always assumed that the club was so consumed by grief at my father's death that they hadn't been thinking clearly. I still didn't understand it.

"Obviously you've got a reason to guard yourself close, when you feel more comfortable you can tell me exactly what happened," he said firmly. "Meanwhile, anyone fucks with you, they fuck with us," he glowered before his expression lightened. "And something tells me my boy won't mind keepin' an eye on you," he added with a mischievous smile that looked just like his son's.

I blushed, unable to look at Cole.

"She's already keeping me busy, Pop," Cole said with a chuckle, earning a narrowed glance from me. "Let's get your apartment sorted darlin'," Cole suggested while heading toward me.

I nodded, still feeling tongue tied. "Thank you," I said simply to Cal, unable to say anything else.

"You got it," he replied firmly. "I've got some more photos and some damn good stories when you got a mind to hear them," he said with a smile and a twinkle in his eye.

"I'd like that," I replied hoarsely, as Cole put an arm around my shoulder and started guiding me outside.

Cal gave me a chin lift as he stood braced against the pool table watching us leave.

I let Cole take my hand in his as he led us to his bike. I was completely shell-shocked, not only at everything that Cal had said, but that Cole and I had known each other when we were children. What were the odds that we would meet randomly, but then share this type of history? My capacity for trust was severely limited, but there was a large part of me that wanted to trust Cal and Cole, to believe that Cal had loved my father and was still devoted to him. I tried to get a grip as we roared off toward my place, focusing on the need for a long, warm shower and a change of clothes. Beyond that, I couldn't focus on much. I could sense Cole's contemplative mood as well as the warm breeze slid over us on the ride.

Cole pulled up to the curb and swung a leg over his bike while holding a hand out to me. He kept a hold of my hand as he led me to my door, gesturing for me to stay outside so he could check out the place before returning to gesture me inside.

"I'll be back soon," he told me simply when he established that I was safe.

"What?" I asked, confused.

He grasped my neck and squeezed it in that now familiar gesture, and left me standing in my living room in surprise. Coming back for what? I shook my head, unable to process anything and headed for the shower.

I stood under the blissfully hot water trying to get a handle on myself. The day had taken a very surprising turn and had dredged up a lot of emotion that I wasn't prepared for.

I heard the front door close and cocked my head to the side to listen.

"Scar?" I heard Kat's voice call.

"Yeah, come in," I hollered in response.

She opened the bathroom door and leaned against the counter as I continued my shower, something we did frequently. Neither one of us was modest in the least.

"What's going on?" she asked, sitting on the closed toilet seat lid.

"What isn't going on," I said, as I proceeded to fill her in on my bizarre morning.

"Holy shit!" she exclaimed when I was done. "I can't believe you two played together when you were young," she marveled, pulling out the one detail that shocked me the most as well.

"I know," I replied. "He said he's coming back. I'm not sure what for or what to do with any of this. Just trying to focus on getting my hair clean for now," I said dryly.

She laughed. "That's a good start. I'll leave you to it," she added before leaving the bathroom.

When I emerged a little while later feeling slightly refreshed, I was shocked to find Cole squatted in front of our door installing a new lock.

"What are you doing?" I asked, surprised.

He looked over at me briefly, his eyes raking over me, reminding me that I was only dressed in my short, terry cloth robe. I pulled it tighter and continued to stare at him, ignoring his cocky grin.

"I'm installing new locks, sweetheart. The last one was shit anyway," he muttered. "And Sal, my buddy from the club, will be over in a few to install an alarm," he added, making my eyes bulge.

"What? That's not necessary!" I protested. "And Kat and I don't have the money for that," I added.

"Good thing you're not paying for it then," he mumbled, turning back to his task at hand.

I scowled and huffed off to my room, knowing I couldn't say or do anything to detract him. I threw myself on my bed and stared up at the ceiling for what felt like an eternity, listening to Sal installing a new alarm system. I could hear Kat chatting with him good naturedly and admired her ability to take almost everything in stride.

"Come in," I answered mindlessly when a soft knock sounded at my door and I assumed it was Kat. Instead, it was Cole who came in and shut the door behind him. I didn't have the energy to tell him to get out, even when he lay down on the bed beside me, throwing an arm casually underneath his head as though he'd done this a thousand times.

I absolutely shocked myself when I rolled toward him, put my head on his chest, and threw an arm over his stomach. It was an action I completed before I even thought about it. Something about him exuded comfort, and I needed that so badly that I couldn't be sorry even after I came to my senses. His other arm came up to stroke my damp hair and we lay like that for an immeasurable amount of time without speaking.

"You should eat something," he said after a while.

"Later," I sighed, too content to move. I finally felt relaxed and wasn't in any rush to change the feeling.

"What time do you have to work?" he asked.

"Five," I groaned.

"Till when?"

"Closing, around one," I answered him.

I felt him stiffen slightly. "You always work those kinds of hours?"

"No," I said. "But the tips are best with the night crowd, so I take it when the opportunity presents itself," I explained softly as he continued to stroke my hair.

"You wanna tell me who you think broke in here last night?" he asked, his voice deceptively soft.

I lifted my head and met his serious gaze, now aware of how close his lips were to mine, how good his body felt underneath me. "I think I've met my quota of sharing for the day," I replied quietly as he gazed up at me.

"I'll give you that for today," he allowed.

"Gee, thanks," I said as I forced a sarcastic smile.

He ignored my flippant tone and stared up at me, his hand still drifting through my hair. I shocked myself yet again by leaning in and pressing my lips to his. I'd never made the first move with a guy before. I figured I'd had a rough few days, so I could allow myself this, even if it meant that I had to steel my resolve against him later. History or no history, I was far more comfortable with the wall I'd built snugly around myself.

His grip tightened in my hair as his lips opened, his tongue meeting mine. It was just seconds before he rolled us so that he was on top taking control of the kiss in a way that nearly devastated me. I'd never been kissed like this. My entire body began to hum and tingle as our tongues tangled in the most natural, yet exhilarating, way. I was suddenly very aware that I was wearing only a robe, and I found myself hoping he would dive into it to explore. Something told me that Cole would be able to make my body feel things that I'd never felt before. My hand slid up underneath his shirt, wanting to touch his bare skin. He groaned softly as my hand explored the contours of his muscles and surprisingly soft skin.

"Cole! I'm done man," Sal hollered from the living room breaking the moment.

"Shit," Cole breathed, his lips against mine. We were both breathing hard as he leaned back to look at me. He traced my lower lip with his thumb before he reluctantly hauled himself off of me and stalked out of the room to talk with Sal.

I took a moment to collect myself. My heart was hammering in my chest, my nipples were aching, and I couldn't believe how damp I was in between my legs just from kissing. I sat up and quickly threw on my clothes, trying to convince myself I was grateful that the moment had been broken before I allowed something more to happen.

I emerged from the bedroom fully dressed as Sal was issuing his final instructions.

"Sal, this is Scarlet," Cole introduced.

Sal looked over at me and gave me a chin lift. He was incredibly handsome, with jet black hair and dark eyes. He had slightly olive skin and a few days worth of scruff. A tattoo snaked its way out of his T-shirt and up his neck.

Kat generally liked preppy guys, but there weren't many women who wouldn't be attracted to Sal. My eyes swung to her and I suddenly realized why she'd been so eager to chat him up. She shrugged at me and winked. I stifled a laugh. A quick last sweep of his attire confirmed that he was part of the MC as well.

"Thanks for doing this," I replied awkwardly.

"Not a problem," his deep voice rumbled.

He headed out after giving Kat a quick nod. She blushed in response – something I'd never seen her do.

Shit. The last thing we needed was to have two broken hearts under one roof.

Cole took the time to show Kat and me the alarm system, making us repeat back his instructions over and over again until we were both rolling our eyes.

Once satisfied, Cole grabbed his jacket. "I'll see you later, got shit to do," he told me swiftly and grasped my neck. But this time, he accompanied the squeeze with a soft, swift kiss.

No way. There shouldn't be a 'later.' This was a good place to call it quits.

"Um, what do you mean 'later?'" I asked quietly.

He looked down at me with amusement. "I mean I'll see you later," he replied, his voice barely above a whisper. That tone wreaked serious havoc on me.

"Um, I'm working later and then I'm sleeping. So maybe we should just…" I drifted off suddenly nervous.

He just chuckled and shook his head, giving me another neck squeeze.

"Later, Kat," he called over his shoulder as if I hadn't spoken.

"Later," she replied, fighting back laughter as he left.

"Don't even say it," I ordered sternly, spinning to face her.

"Scar, there's so much to say I wouldn't even know where to start!" She grinned from ear to ear.

I scowled, knowing she was right and went to get ready for work.

My shift went by quickly and I was grateful for the distraction. Rushing from table to table and remembering food and drink orders didn't allow for much else to fill my head, though I did manage to think of Cole and that kiss about a thousand times.

It was winding down around midnight, and Connie and I were taking a breather when a blond girl with huge breasts and bright red lipstick came striding into Jupiter.

"Oh shit," Connie muttered.

"Who's that?" I asked, perplexed when it was clear that the girl was headed right for us.

"One of Cole's old hook ups, just ignore her," Connie replied with disdain.

Shit.

"You Scarlet?" The girl sneered.

"Yep," I answered, standing up straight and meeting her judgmental gaze. If this girl thought I was someone who could be easily fucked with, then she had another thing coming. It was a common misperception about me – people always thought I was sheltered and soft. It wasn't until they rubbed me the wrong way that they discovered what I was really made of.

"Stay the fuck away from Cole, he's mine," she warned.

I laughed right in her face. "Honey, you might want to pass your message along to Cole if you're concerned about it. I'm not the one doing the chasing," I replied, completely unaffected by her. I'd dealt with this type of woman time and time again and they were all the same. Thought they could sleep with a guy in the club and then sink their claws in. There were the kind of girls who became old ladies, and then there were the ones who were one-night stands. This girl was clearly the latter.

"I don't give a fuck who's doing the chasing. Stay away from him!" she cried, agitated that I wasn't taking her seriously.

"Don't raise your voice when you walk into my place of work," I replied, finally aggravated with her. "If you think with all the other shit I've got going on that you remotely concern me, you have another thing coming. But I will tell you one thing, you continue to stand there and threaten me, you'll be the one who has something to be concerned about. Now get the fuck out of my bar," I said, staring her down with fire in my eyes.

She glared at me clearly trying to gauge how serious I was. Whatever she saw in my expression, it sent her flouncing back in the direction she'd come from with an audible huff.

"Holy shit, I had no idea you were such a badass!" Connie squealed, laughing hysterically. "That was the best thing I've seen in my entire life!" she hooted.

I shrugged, suddenly feeling tired.

Her expression immediately softened when she saw how exhausted I was. "Hey, things are slow. Why don't you take off?" she offered. "I don't know the extent of what's going on, but you look like you could use an extra hour of sleep," she offered kindly.

"You know what? I absolutely could," I agreed. "I owe you one, thank you," I replied sincerely.

"Don't mention it. And you don't owe me anything, that little encounter was all the pay back I need," she said.

I laughed lightly and reached behind the bar to grab my purse.

I drove home with the welcome thought of my soft bed, hoping that tomorrow would feel more like a normal day. What I certainly didn't need was any more biker drama.

It took me a minute to remember the alarm code when I got home, but I managed to turn it off and reset it before the National Guard was called. Kat wasn't home, not a surprise since she was always off doing something. I got ready for bed, donned my typical camisole and shorts, and sighed blissfully when my head hit the pillow. I had to admit, the new alarm and locks were reassuring and I didn't have any trouble drifting off.

My phone rang and woke me up after what felt like just seconds of sleep. I squinted and saw "Cole calling" flashing on the screen. Of course he programmed himself into my phone. I hit ignore and drifted back to sleep. My phone rang again, not a moment later, and I picked it up knowing he wouldn't stop until I did.

"Yeah?" I asked, my voice raspy with sleep.

"What the fuck, babe?" his deep voice demanded through the phone.

"Hello to you too," I answered dryly.

"I thought you had to work till one, Wes was supposed to make sure you got home okay, but you weren't there."

"Is it a crime for a girl to get off early? Jesus calm down," I grumbled irritably.

He sighed, clearly trying to get a handle on his temper. "I was just concerned, that's all."

Now was an excellent time to say what I'd intended to

earlier, even if I was half asleep.

"Cole, I appreciate everything you've done, but this isn't your concern. I don't expect, nor do I want, any type of protection. Whatever obligation you feel toward me, it's not necessary."

"You think its obligation that I feel?" he growled.

"I don't know what it is that you feel, and frankly, the visit I got at work tonight just confirmed that I don't want to know," I replied harshly. Okay, maybe this was the point where I realized that having this conversation half asleep was a bad idea. My snarky side seemed to be wide awake, though.

"I heard about that. It's been dealt with," he replied without hesitation.

I laughed. "Something tells me there's more than one of those girls waiting in the wings. Were you planning on chartering a blimp to broadcast some type of message?" I asked sarcastically. "She was classy by the way, good to know what your type is."

He chuckled unaffected by the bite of my words. "If you didn't care what it is that I feel, then you wouldn't give a shit. From the sound of your voice it seems that she got you all riled up. And from what Connie said, it was a sight to see, too. So from where I sit, you're just denying the inevitable with your suit of armor darlin'," he drawled.

I scowled that he had me pegged.

"I'm surprisingly patient, so you can keep up this act a while longer if you'd like, though I really don't see the point."

"God, you are infuriating," I seethed.

He chuckled, his deep voice sending a wave of tingles straight to my groin in a way I wished I could deny. "Yeah, but you like it, all of it," he replied arrogantly.

God, I so did. Dammit.

"Are you going to keep goading me or are you going to let me sleep?" I demanded.

"You set the alarm? Lock the doors?" he asked, his tone softer now.

"Yes," I sighed.

"Okay then. I'll pick you up at six tomorrow night."

"Wait, what?" I demanded.

"Already checked with Connie, I know you don't have to work. You and I are going out. I would tell you what to wear, but I'm sure anything you chose will be sexy as hell. Night darlin'," he murmured before he hung up.

"Gah!" He clearly wasn't accepting my brush off and I wasn't entirely certain what to do about that. The man drove me absolutely crazy, in every way.

Chapter Four

I considered standing Cole up, I really did. But then I thought about everything he'd already done for me, and I couldn't go through with it. And if I was being honest with myself, I was thrilled at the prospect of spending more time with him. It was official, I was a glutton for punishment.

After some guesswork and lots of input from Kat the next evening, I settled on tight, dark blue jeans and my green fitted blouse that hugged my curves and made my eyes pop. I finished it off with my high heeled sandals. It was an outfit that would work in almost any setting, which was pretty much what I had to go for. I left my long hair down and a bit wild. To complete the look, I applied black eyeliner and my blush colored lipstick for a bit of color.

"You look smoking," Kat assured me with a grin when I twirled for her.

"For someone who makes you so irritated you sure do seem excited to see him," she teased.

"Shut it," I warned.

"Why are you still trying to push the poor guy away?" she asked innocently. "Ever since you discovered that you guys have a shared history, I thought you might be a bit more open to the idea," she added.

The truth was that I'd considered this fact as well. It was true that having a shared history and having talked to his father did make me trust him more. But that didn't mean he still wasn't a seasoned womanizer. I was now more intent on protecting my heart than worrying about my safety. And I told Kat as much.

She smiled sympathetically. "Honey, sometimes we gotta just put ourselves out there," she encouraged.

"Yeah, well that hasn't always worked out so well for me," I grumbled.

"First time for everything," she grinned as we heard his bike rumble to a stop in front of our place.

A knock at the door came moments later, and I opened it to find Cole looking beautiful as always on the other side. He wore his typical uniform – a leather jacket, jeans, and motorcycle boots. He looked good enough to eat. His eyes drifted leisurely over my figure before he cocked a brow and held out a woman's leather jacket.

"You're gonna need one of these," he said as he grinned. "I guessed the size, hopefully it fits."

It took me a moment before I reached out to grab it. "Thank you," I replied, shocked at the gesture, and put it on over my blouse. It was a tight fit over my ample chest, and I gave him a wry smile. "I'm guessing that wasn't an accident."

"Nope," he chuckled, his eyes lighting up as he took me in. "It suits you."

"We'll see," I muttered, waving good-bye to Kat and following him outside.

"Where are we going anyway?" I asked as I put on the helmet he'd handed me.

"Dinner," he answered simply with a wry smile, turning the bike on as I wrapped my arms around his waist.

I was surprised when we pulled into Gunny's, a very well-regarded steak joint just outside of town. It was on the pricey side, so I'd never eaten there, but I'd certainly heard about it.

"Am I dressed okay for this place?" I asked a bit worriedly, running a hand nervously over my blouse.

"You look beautiful," he assured me, taking my hand and leading me inside with a confidence I found incredibly attractive.

The host showed us to a quiet booth along the window and I suddenly felt nervous as we sat across from each other. I hadn't been on an actual date in years and I started to feel unsure of myself.

"You look nervous," Cole observed while grinning at me, completely at ease and in his element, which seemed to be the case no matter where we were.

"I guess I am a little," I admitted.

"Why?"

I shrugged. "It's been a while since I was on a date," I admitted.

"How long's a while?" he wanted to know, eyeing me intently.

"Years," I murmured.

His brows rose to his hairline. "Years? How is that possible?" he demanded.

There were a lot of ways to answer that question. "I'm picky," I said, settling for the easiest. It was true.

He chuckled. "Well, I'm glad to hear it."

I was tempted to quip that I wished he'd been picky as well, but I bit my tongue. Damn that snarky side. He seemed to bring it out in me.

The waiter came and we ordered our drinks. I ordered a cocktail and Cole stuck with beer.

"We're having a barbecue at the club tomorrow, you should come," he said as I sipped the drink that had just been placed in front of me.

"I don't think that's a good idea," I replied resolutely.

"Why not? You know I'd never let anything happen to you, right?" he asked, staring at me intently.

And oddly enough, I did know that, I just didn't understand it. Nor was that my main concern about the barbecue. I took a deep breath before plunging in. "Listen, Cole," I began, choosing my words carefully, "I grew up in a club just like you. I know how things work, and I know how the men in the club are," I told him, ignoring the narrowing of his eyes. "I don't think this is a good idea," I finished with a shake of my head.

"So you're just going to throw me in with that lot?" he demanded, clearly frustrated.

I pegged him with a knowing stare. "And you're going to tell me that you haven't had countless women in your bed?" I demanded. "That you have more one-night stands than not? That's just not for me," I shook my head.

"That's a hell of an assumption," he growled.

"Am I wrong?" I countered with raised brows.

He sighed and I knew I'd hit my mark. He was silent for a moment as he regarded me intently. "It's different with you," he said finally. I had to admit that his expression was utterly sincere.

"Why?" I demanded skeptically as he rudely waved away the waiter who'd come to take our order. "Why are you so protective over some girl you just met?" I demanded, watching the waiter back away.

"What do you think?" he asked with a tilt of his head.

When I didn't reply he sighed. "I'm probably this way with you for the same reason that you're going on a date with me when you haven't gone on one for years. There are exceptions to every rule. How about we leave it at that for now?" he suggested, his gaze still intent on my face.

I bit my lip and thought about that. He'd made a fair point: he was different for me. I supposed there was a teensy possibility I was for him as well. "Fair enough," I allowed.

He sighed, seeming relieved that we could move on and sat casually back in his seat. "So how about the barbecue?" he asked again, bringing the subject back when I thought I'd successfully derailed him.

"You're asking me to put myself on the grid," I practically whispered.

I saw several emotions pass over his face, but the one I saw the strongest was possession. I knew he wanted fiercely to protect me. I didn't doubt that.

He reached out and took my hand over the table, squeezing lightly. "Baby, you don't think you already are?" he asked gently.

My eyes widened as I considered what I'd been denying for the last few days. "For now I'm going to play the part of an optimist," I said as I tried to smile. "It's new for me, we'll see how it goes."

He smiled at my attempt of lightheartedness.

"Can we let the poor man take our order?" I quipped when I saw our waiter making his way back over to us, desperate to change the topic. I took my hand back and placed it in my lap.

"I suppose," Cole smiled, forcing his tone to lighten.

We talked easily for the rest of the meal about relatively frivolous topics – music and movies we liked, our close friends, favorite spots to eat. I was surprised to learn that he was quite a reader, and we spent a fair amount of time on books.

"Want to go shoot some pool for a little bit?" he asked when he'd settled the bill. I nodded, not wanting the evening to end just yet.

"Thanks for dinner, it was delicious." I smiled sincerely, hoping it hadn't cost too much.

"You're welcome," he grinned, throwing an arm around me as we walked to his bike.

We rode to a bar I'd never been to before close to downtown. It was a total dive, but that suited me just fine. He ordered us a couple of beers and we started playing a game of pool. I hadn't played in years, but we'd had a table at my dad's club and I wasn't a slouch.

"You're pretty good for a girl," Cole said as he smirked at me over the table, looking impossibly gorgeous in his tight black T-shirt. His eyes shined in the dim light as he leaned against his cue.

"You did not just say that." I narrowed my eyes at him.

"I may have," he allowed playfully.

"You won't be so cocky when I kick your ass," I retorted, my competitive streak coming out with a vengeance.

Snarky and competitive, wow I was really laying on the charm with him.

"Oh really?" He cocked a brow. "How about we make this interesting and make a bet?"

"Fine." I never could turn down a dare.

"I win, you come to the barbecue. You win, I might

let you kiss me at the end of the night," he said, clearly enjoying himself.

"No deal," I scoffed with a laugh.

He sighed in mock exasperation. "Fine. I win, you let me spend the night. No expectations," he added when my eyes got wide. "You win…"

"You wash my car and take out our trash this week," I butted in.

He laughed. "Fine, deal."

We got down to it and I was off to a great start. I definitely used my cleavage to my advantage when I bent over, as well as any good angle I could leverage when he was behind me. I heard him suck in his breath a few times and I grinned to myself. But then he hit a roll, and before I knew it, he was sinking the eight ball victoriously.

"Dammit," I muttered.

"Don't worry, darlin'. I'll stick to my side of the bed," he said with a wink.

"No one said anything about us sharing a bed." I smiled sweetly. "You should be more specific with your bets," I pointed out.

He merely grinned and headed off to use the bathroom.

I found a table and sat down, sipping my second beer and realizing that this was the best date I'd ever been on. Aside from the slightly strained start of dinner, the rest of the evening had been light and fun. It felt very natural to be with him. The frequent stomach flutters weren't so bad either.

"Buy you another?" a deep voice asked as I looked up at a scruffy looking biker.

"No thanks," I shook my head.

"How about a game then?" he asked, gesturing to the

pool tables.

"I'm here with someone," I replied firmly.

"I don't see anyone." He shrugged, making an arrogant show of looking around.

"Then you should look behind you asshole," Cole's voice rumbled from behind him.

"Shit, Jackson. Sorry man. I didn't realize," the guy apologized when he got a look at the very angry man behind him. He obviously knew Cole and clearly knew he had seriously fucked up.

"Get lost, now." Cole glowered angrily.

The guy threw up his hands in a gesture of apology and walked away. I shot a hesitant smile up at Cole, trying to assess his mood.

"Can't leave you for a second," he mumbled while sitting down next to me.

"I've fended for myself pretty well for twenty six years," I reminded him. "Plus that guy was harmless," I waved my hand in a casual gesture while taking a sip of my beer.

"I still don't like it," he grumbled.

"Do you want to go?" I asked when it seemed clear his mood wasn't going to improve.

He simply nodded and we stood to put on our jackets.

"Hey," I said softly, putting my hands on his chest and looking up at him. "Don't let two minutes ruin what was otherwise a great date," I said, meeting his fierce gaze.

His expression softened considerably as he put his hands gently on either side of my face. He was capable of a tenderness I'd never experienced before, and I shuddered a bit as he put his lips softly to mine.

"Deal," he murmured as he pressed his forehead to mine.

I smiled, taking the hand he offered and followed him out of the bar and to his bike.

My stomach tightened with anxiety when we turned onto my street, wondering what the night would bring with him staying over. It was, technically speaking, our first date, but I doubted I'd have much restraint if I was sharing a bed with him. My head and my body seemed to have a difference of opinion when it came to Cole.

When he pulled the bike to the curb I turned in surprise when he showed no signs of getting off.

"Not on a bet," he shook his head, his eyes smoldering into mine.

"What?" I demanded, surprised at how disappointed I was.

He grinned at my clear frustration. "Not on a bet," he reiterated. "You invite me in, it'll be because you want me to spend the night with you. Not because you lost a bet. And darlin', that day will come soon. I'm not worried about it," he said as he winked at me.

God, he was so infuriating. Not only was he now denying me what I'd started to look forward to, but he was maddeningly arrogant.

"Suit yourself," I huffed.

"Come here, babe," he requested quietly, still straddling his bike.

I went to him. When I was in reaching distance, his arm snaked around my waist and pulled me flush against him. "You've got the sweetest mouth," he murmured, pressing his lips to mine. I made a low noise in my throat and the kiss took on a life of its own. His tongue slid into my mouth, sending tingles down my spine and legs, and his hand slid into my hair pulling gently. I wrapped my arms around his shoulders and gave him everything I had with a kind of abandon I didn't know was in me.

"Shit, I have to go now," he growled, pulling free of me, his eyes shouldering.

I nodded, feeling slightly shaky on my feet.

"Sleep well," he said, starting the bike up again as I backed away.

"You, too." I smiled and watched him as he roared off down my street.

Apparently the sidewalk had turned to air as I walked to my apartment. My limbs seemed to move independently from the rest of my body as I turned off the alarm and began to get ready for bed. I'd never felt so completely blissed out in my entire life. I fell asleep smiling, something I'd never done before. I still had my hesitations about Cole and there was still so much to consider, but in that moment after such a great night, all I could think about was how happy he made me.

Chapter Five

I woke up to the alarm clanging loudly throughout our apartment. It took me a moment to place it before ice slid through my veins. I prayed it was just Kat forgetting the code, but deep down I knew differently. I grabbed the baseball bat I kept underneath the bed and opened my bedroom door hesitantly. Kat was doing the same, and I gave her a wide-eyed look. Clearly someone else had triggered the alarm. The front door stood wide open and my heart hammered loudly in my veins. I took a quick visual sweep of the apartment. Whoever had tried to get in, the alarm must have scared them off. I went over and turned it off, my hands shaking so much that it took me a couple of tries.

"We have to call the police, Scar," Kat whispered behind me, her eyes wide.

"I know," I sighed in resignation.

"I'll put my name on the statement," she said, trying to assure me.

"They'll still want mine, too. It's okay. It's inevitable," I sighed. Plus, I had to face the fact that the person I'd been avoiding all this time and the break-ins were probably related anyway. The thought was not a comforting one.

The police showed up fifteen minutes later, two cars and three officers. It felt overwhelming to have so much attention, and I shivered in my shorts and cami, wishing I'd thought to put on a robe.

I was dumbfounded when Cole stalked into the apartment as the police were finishing up our statements. He eyed me for a moment before disappearing into my room and returning with my robe. I gratefully pulled it around myself and looked up at him beyond relieved, if not surprised to see him.

"What are you doing here?" I asked quietly.

"We'll talk later," he replied firmly, turning to one of the officers to ask for details. Their conversation was just a blur of sound to me as I tried to make sense of everything that was happening.

I realized with a jolt that I should just leave town. As much as it pained me, I was bringing nothing but trouble for Kat and now for Cole.

"I'm stayin'," Cole said firmly once the police had taken their reports and pulled away in their cars. The apartment felt eerily quiet with all the commotion over.

I saw Kat sag with relief at Cole's decree and I nodded, grateful to have his presence as well.

"What do we do about the door?" I asked, looking at the now splintered front door.

He looked down at the baseball bat by my feet and took it over to the door wedging it underneath the handle forcing it closed. "Anyone opens it, the alarm will sound, but I doubt anyone would dare with my bike parked out front," he said confidently.

He was probably right. And I couldn't deny that I was relieved to have someone else take care of things for a change. I hadn't known Cole long, but I already trusted him, something beyond rare for me.

"Bed, babe," he said softly, taking in my frazzled state.

I nodded before turning to Kat. "I'm so sorry Kat," I whispered, my voice hoarse with emotion.

"Don't you ever say you're sorry. This is not your fault. I won't ever accept that type of apology. Got it?" she demanded. Kat had already done so much for me and now I was bringing my shit directly to her door. There was no way I couldn't be sorry, but I knew her well enough to bite my tongue.

I nodded without speaking and headed off to my room. I heard Cole speak to her for a few moments as I crawled back underneath the covers, but I couldn't hear what they said. He entered the room moments later, ditching his jacket, shirt, and jeans –leaving him in nothing but boxers. I was too upset to appreciate the view, which was unfortunate.

He crawled into bed and didn't hesitate pulling me against him.

"How did you know?" I asked quietly, resting my head on his firm chest. His skin was warm and he smelled amazing. My senses were rapidly returning it seemed.

"Wes did a drive by," he explained. "Why didn't you call?" he demanded lightly.

The thought honestly hadn't even occurred to me. "Because it's the middle of the night and we've been on one date," I replied, clearly baffled by his question.

"You're so not getting this," he muttered, but didn't elaborate.

I lifted my head and looked him in the eye. "I'm gonna leave town, Cole. It's for the best," I said softly.

His eyes narrowed and his grip on the back of my neck tightened.

"I've been patient and tried to let you figure it out in your own time, but clearly that isn't gonna happen," he sighed, exasperated. "Babe, I've staked my claim. You're mine. You've been mine since you got on the back of my bike," he decreed.

My eyes widened in shock.

"You know it, I know you do. You're the exception to my rule," he whispered, roughly giving me another neck squeeze and bringing his forehead to mine.

And I realized that I did know that, I'd been fighting it, but I knew it. And while part of me wanted to squeal with joy, the other part felt complete trepidation.

"All this shit, it's not your responsibility or your fault," he continued. "We got word that fucker Jake and some others are making plays against us," he informed me. "I'd a been in this shit whether you were here or not. You've just proved to be a damn good way to get us riled," he muttered.

That did make me feel better I had to admit. But I was still confused.

"So this isn't just Jake trying to fuck with me?" I asked, my brows furrowed. It's what I'd assumed all along.

I felt Cole's entire body stiffen, we hadn't talked about the details, but I assumed his father had filled him in on my history, the pieces he knew anyway.

"I don't doubt he's fucking with you sweetheart," his deep voice rumbled. "But there's a lot more to it than just that," he explained. "And for now, the less you know, probably the better," he added.

I nodded, surprisingly fine with that.

"So no more talk of leaving town or apologizing to your best friend for that piece of shit," he said, firmly looking intently into my eyes. He doesn't deserve anything of yours, not one fucking thing, but especially not fucking guilt. You get that?" he demanded.

I nodded. "Yeah, I get it," I said softly before I cleared my throat for what I had to ask next. "How much do you know?"

Whatever he saw in my expression made his eyes soften as they looked back into mine. Clearly he understood what I was getting at. "Enough. Not what's in your head or what you remember, of course. But I know your father was a good man who did the best he could when your mama died," he said softly as I bit back the emotion that was growing in my chest, threatening to suffocate me. "I know that Jake fucking Silvera had something to do with him getting killed. I also know that Jake and you had something when you were kids that obviously he thought more of since he expected you to be at his side when he took over runnin' the club. Clearly you had other ideas, because you split the first chance you got," he said, and I thought I detected a hint of pride in his tone. "And I know that you're as hard as nails as you are soft and sweet, and you've got something I want not only to protect, but selfishly something I want for myself, too," he murmured while kissing my forehead.

Wow, that was sweet. I sagged into him unable to convey with words how much gratitude and longing I felt for him in that moment. He was unlike any of the men I'd grown up with. He had a hard edge for sure, but his heart was as warm as they came.

"Sleep, babe everything's gonna be fine," he assured me.

"K," I muttered.

"Can Kat come to the barbecue, too?" I muttered, half asleep.

I was sure I felt him smile. "Yeah, babe."

Then it was lights out.

I woke up feeling warm and I smiled when I felt the wall of Cole behind me. He was pressed to my back yet again with an arm thrown over my waist, pulling me close. I'd never been with someone who liked to cuddle, and it was a welcomed change. My skin began to hum with the awareness of him and I grinned as I scooted my behind that much closer to his boxer covered body. He growled softly in response, and his arm got tighter around me. My whole body lit up as I rolled to face him. His eyes were wide open, sleep only a memory as his gaze bore down into mine. His hand trailed down my torso, clenching at my waist and I could tell it was taking all of his restraint from launching himself at me.

I looked him over, my eyes hungrily devouring his form and thought, fuck it. I sat up and slowly pulled my camisole over my head.

I saw his eyes widen in response, his pupils dilated and his nostrils flared. It was the most animalistic response I'd ever seen in a man before, and it sent a rush of wetness between my legs.

"You are the sexiest fucking thing I've ever seen," his deep voice rumbled as he did in fact launch at me, throwing his body over mine. He pulled me into a passionate kiss as his hands trailed like liquid fire down my smooth back and into my shorts, cupping my ass.

"You have no idea how much I've wanted to have my hands on this ass," he groaned, squeezing me firmly.

I sighed in response as his hands pulled my shorts down and off my legs.

His mouth trailed from my mouth to my neck and further still until it reached one of my nipples. I heard my own intake of breath when he took one in his mouth and sucked, nibbling slightly until I was fighting back a loud groan. It occurred to me absently that Kat was home and that the walls were by no means thick.

His mouth continued its exploration as he moved down past my breasts to my stomach and further until he reached his goal. I'd never felt that comfortable with having a man's mouth on me, but there was something so erotic about watching Cole and the hungry look in his eye when he looked up at me, that all thought of modesty fled my brain. He pulled my legs apart forcefully and dove in like a man starved.

"Oh, God," I breathed softly as he sucked and nibbled until my legs were shaking and I could feel my body building up to something mind blowing. It was mere moments before it washed over me as sweat broke out across my brow and I had to throw my arm across my mouth so I didn't cry out.

It was then that we both heard the front door open and Kat's car start up.

"Thank fucking Christ," Cole muttered, his mouth sending incredible sensation down my inner thigh.

I pulled him up toward me and pulled his boxers off with both feet. "Tell me you're on the pill," he said, his tone desperate as he looked down at me.

"I'm on the pill," I replied without hesitation.

"I've never not used a condom, not ever. But I don't want to use one with you. Do you trust me?" he asked quietly.

"I trust you," I nodded. And I did. It was shocking what I would trust this man with.

He kissed me then, long and deep before I felt him slide inside me.

"Ah," I protested only slightly.

"Baby, you are so fucking tight," he rumbled, his lips at my ear. "I'll go slow until you get used to me."

"Okay," I replied breathlessly.

He slowed his rhythm, gently sliding in and out until I only felt pleasure and no pain.

"I've got it now," I told him, my hands gripping his firm shoulders.

"Christ you feel good," he groaned as he picked up the pace.

I'd never felt anything like this before. I'd had sex before, but I realized I hadn't come close to experiencing the full potential of the act. With Cole's body moving inside and over mine, I immediately began to feel a quickening that I'd never felt before.

"Oh, God," I cried out, feeling almost afraid of what was about to happen. It felt so intense, like I wouldn't be able to handle it.

"Let it go, baby," he commanded gently.

As it turned out, I didn't have much choice in the matter, and my orgasm washed over me in a rush as I clenched around him, my nails raking his back. I didn't even recognize my own voice as I cried out. I absently heard him groan with his own release into me before he collapsed on top of me, breathing hard into my neck.

After a few moments he rolled off, lying on his side so we were facing each other. His hand stroked the curve of my hip as we looked at each other.

I blushed and let a small giggle escape, making his face light up.

"Now she's blushing," he muttered, making me laugh. "You okay?" he asked, his face serious. "I would have been gentler, I didn't realize..." he trailed off.

"That I've been a nun for a few years?" I teased. "I'm great Cole, amazing," I assured him.

"Good," he sighed, squeezing my hip.

"Good that I was a nun?" I teased him. Our light hearted moments seemed so few and far between that I relished them when they happened.

"That too," he grinned, kissing me again.

"Shit," I swore, realizing what time it was. "I have to get ready for work," I said, sitting up and running my fingers through my wild mane of hair. From behind, I felt his warm hand caress my naked back reverently.

"Then let's take a shower," he suggested, his lips against my shoulder.

I shivered slightly. The thought of taking a shower was certainly tempting.

"Okay," I grinned, turning my face to his and kissing him softly.

We padded naked to the bathroom and I was shocked that I didn't feel more self-conscious being completely naked in front of him in broad daylight. It certainly helped that every time I caught him looking at me it was with such blatant appreciation that it was clear he liked what he saw.

"You have the most beautiful body I've ever seen," he murmured, reaffirming my earlier thoughts as we stood in the shower with the warm water cascading over us. His hands trailed down my arms and over my hips as though he wanted to appreciate every inch of me. "Not gonna lie, I spent a lot of nights thinkin' about what you look like. And baby, you surpassed my expectations," he admitted as he grinned.

"Stop," I pleaded, blushing. I didn't admit out loud that the same was true for me as well. Cole's body was breathtaking. My hands moved appreciatively over his expansive chest to the six pack below. The man was seriously cut. The raw strength emanating from him was overwhelmingly hot.

He kissed me then, his tongue sliding over my lips with a gentle request for me to open to him. I obeyed immediately and melted into him as our tongues tangled. I'd never showered with a man before and so far it was safe to say that I was thoroughly enjoying the experience.

His fingers continued their exploration, moving to more intimate areas of my body as he flitted them teasingly over each nipple.

I sucked in a breath and pushed myself into his hands.

"So impatient," he murmured with a smile.

"Nun, remember?" I answered breathlessly as his hand slipped between my legs.

His hardness strained between us as he slipped two fingers inside me. My hands clenched onto his strong forearms in response as my legs began to shake underneath me.

"So wet already," his deep voice rumbled with pleasure. "I like that, baby."

I kissed him passionately in response, my fingers twisting into his hair. My hand traveled down his body as I took him into my hand. He sucked in a harsh breath and grabbed my ass with his free hand. He continued to work between my legs until I was panting and completely lost to his touch.

"Hop up darlin'," he directed, pulling my ass up so that my legs wrapped around his waist.

"Oh shit," I said and I sucked in a breath as he pressed me into the wall and slid inside me with one thrust.

"Tell me if it's too much," he rasped, forcing himself not to move.

My body felt deliciously full with him inside of me at this angle and I didn't want him to hold back.

"I will, just give it to me," I practically begged.

"Fuck, just hearing you say that could send me over the edge," he growled as he pulled out almost to the tip and thrust back in with a force that made me cry out. He picked up the tempo, slamming into me much harder than before and I loved each and every second.

My legs began to shake as I tried to control the chaotic sensations he brought out in me.

"Don't fight it," he grunted, pressing deeper still. "I'm close, you with me?"

"Yes," I hissed through my teeth as I climbed higher still. His thrusts intensified and sent me flying over the edge with a force I didn't know was possible.

Seconds later he groaned his own release into me, his lips against my neck.

We stood there for a few moments with my legs still wrapped tightly around him and listened to the sound of the water hitting the tile.

Too soon, he pulled away setting me gently on my feet. He tenderly moved my wet hair back from my face leaning down to kiss me chastely. Only then did we actually get to the business of showering.

In the end I was late for work, but it was well worth it.

Chapter Six

Kat enthusiastically agreed to go the barbecue with me, seeming to enjoy that I was asking her to go out for a change. I told Cole we'd meet him there when we were off work and ready.

"What does one wear to a biker barbecue?" Kat asked with a raised brow as we stared at her closet.

"One wears jeans, or a casual dress and some kick ass sandals or boots," I answered her with a smile. At least in this area I knew what I was talking about. I was already dressed in tight fitted jeans that showed off my backside, a form fitting halter tank top, and ankle boots. I put my hair up in a messy bun, allowing a few chunky pieces to fall around my face.

"Do you think Sal will be there?" she asked innocently once she'd selected her outfit. We were doing our makeup side by side in the bathroom.

I nudged her with my arm. "Took a shine to him did you?" I teased.

"Perhaps." She rolled her eyes.

"I don't know, maybe." I shrugged. "I'm not sure who will be there aside from Wes and Connie. But you know, Kat," I began after a pause, "these guys aren't typically relationship material," I warned. "I just don't want you to get hurt," I explained. I knew Kat could hold her own, she'd always been incredibly confident and feisty. But I'd never seen her take an interest the way she had in Sal and it was my duty as her best friend to warn her.

"I know," she said and smiled at me warmly. I'd always been a bit of a mother hen with her, she was used to it. "I'll proceed with caution," she assured me. "Plus, you know me, since when am I looking for a relationship anyway?" she said as she wrinkled her brow with distaste.

"True," I laughed.

We headed out through the door that Cole had repaired before he'd left that morning. My stomach fluttered with excitement at the thought of seeing him, but I also felt nervous to see his father again and to go to a party at the club. I'd been to a million Sinners' barbecues but that felt like a lifetime ago.

We arrived well after dark and could hear from the street that things were in full swing.

"Here goes," I muttered as we walked toward the building I'd been to once before. But instead of going inside, I did as Cole had instructed and came around the side since everyone was out back. The music was loud but voices and laughter were louder when we reached the back. It was a simple space with a large concrete patio, a couple of picnic tables, and plenty of folding chairs strewn about. There were large fires going in two fire pits, with flames dancing and providing hints of the desert that lay beyond.

The grill was full of meat and the beer was flowing, all in all just what I'd expected. I searched for Cole but didn't see him at first, and I was instantly thankful that Kat was with me. "Let's get a drink," I suggested, heading toward one of the kegs.

"Let me get that for you ladies," an older biker offered, pouring our cups full of beer.

"Thanks, have you seen Cole?" I asked when he handed me my cup.

"Not long ago, over that way," he said, pointing to the back of the building.

I nodded and Kat followed me through the boisterous crowd. It didn't take us long to find him, and my heart dropped at what I saw. He was sitting casually at one of the tables with three other men. But that wasn't where my attention went. There was a blond woman standing next to him, her fingers combing through his hair, her chest provocatively pressed to his shoulder. Clearly they knew each other well, intimately even. And he was doing nothing to dissuade her. The sight of her hands on him made a temper rise up in me that I didn't know I had. I felt sick and like a complete and total fool.

"Shit," I heard Kat mutter.

"We're outta here," I replied, turning on my heel and stalking back to my car. Kat followed without a word, knowing there was no talking me out of it – not that she would try in this situation.

"Hey, Scarlet," Wes greeted stepping in front of us. "Cole's waiting for you."

"Yeah, well he'll continue to fucking wait," I growled. "We gotta go," I told him, unable to temper my rudeness. Wes knit his brows in confusion, but shrugged and let us past.

"Let's go get drunk," I said firmly once we were back at my car.

"Okay," Kat answered quietly. "But Scar, I know that

looked bad but he knew you were coming. If he was going to do something shady, why would he do it while he was waiting for you? She's probably just some hanger-on that he couldn't get rid of," she said, and I was surprised she was coming to his defense.

"I don't care who she was. The fact that he was sitting there letting her touch him like that speaks volumes," I replied angrily, starting my car and roaring off just as my phone started to ring.

"Speak of the devil," I muttered, reaching over to turn it off.

I heard Kat sigh, but she didn't say anything as I drove us downtown. We headed back to Jupiter where the drinks were free and we could hang out with our coworkers.

"Sorry you missed your chance to see Sal," I apologized as we sipped our drinks following the shot that Frank, our bartender, had insisted on. Clearly my car was staying put and we were cabbing it tonight.

"It's okay," she said. "Scar, you at least have to answer that," she pleaded as my phone began to ring again. "He worries," she added.

I narrowed my eyes at her. "Since when did you become Team Cole?" I accused.

"I'm always Team Scarlet, always," she assured me. "But I think he's a good guy. I'd at least hear him out."

"Fine," I grumbled. "I'll be back," I muttered as I slid off my stool at the bar and went outside to take his call.

"Yeah?" I answered.

"Yeah?" he asked incredulously. "Where the fuck are you?" he growled. "Wes said you high-tailed it out of here looking all pissed off."

"It seems I had a change of plans for the evening," I

quipped.

"You had a change of plans," he stated, his voice low with anger. Clearly Cole had never been stood up. He didn't seem to like it much. Well, to fucking bad.

"Yeah, my plans changed when I got all dressed up to come hang out with the guy I slept with twice this morning, only to find some trashy looking chick's hands embedded in his hair with her tits shoved in his face," I hissed.

"That's just Daisy. Jesus babe," he sighed, sounding exasperated, which sent my temper into overdrive.

"That's just Daisy?" I repeated, my voice carefully controlled. I was determined not to lose my cool and start shrieking, though that's exactly what I wanted to do. "I grew up with a lot of Daisy's, Cole. And I'd just about bet my left arm that you've sampled your fair share of Daisy," I said, my tone turning surly every time I said her name. "How do you think it makes me look to walk into your club when you've got your old bed partner wrapped around you? It makes me look like a fucking idiot is what it looks like," I spat before he could interject. "And maybe that's the way you do things, but that sure as fuck doesn't work for me. I'm not going to be yours and not have you be mine. That means that you don't let some girl you've slept with – or any girl for that matter – put her hands on you. Not when you've just invited the girl you're currently sleeping with to come be with you. Not ever!"

Okay, now I was officially shrieking. Dammit.

"And our status as 'currently sleeping together' is now definitely in question," I hissed.

"Are you done?" he asked, his own tone laced with anger.

"Not much else to say," I replied hotly.

"Good, now get your ass back over here," he ordered.

I laughed scornfully. "The hell I will, Cole. Are you high? Did you hear anything I just said?" I demanded.

"I heard everything you just said, respected some of it, too, despite you being hysterical over nothing," he muttered. "Now get your ass over here so I can calm you down properly," he said authoritatively and entirely too sure of himself.

"No way. Kat and I have a date to get drunk and that's what I intend to do. Then maybe we'll find her a guy to exchange numbers with. Then I plan to go to sleep alone," I emphasized. "Have fun at the barbecue. I'm sure Daisy will be more than happy to give you seconds, thirds, or whatever serving you're currently on," I hissed and hung up.

The last part may have been a bit dramatic, but I couldn't help myself. I headed back inside and took my seat next to Kat.

"Well?" she asked.

"I read him the riot act," I muttered, taking a much needed sip of my cocktail to calm my adrenaline. Apparently that was just Daisy," I quipped.

"Oh dear," Kat muttered into her drink.

"Yeah," I muttered back.

We proceeded to drink our cocktails, being handed a second round by the dutiful Frank, and we people watched as usual. We were finally starting to have fun and loosen up when Kat's eyes grew wide as she looked over my shoulder.

"What?" I demanded.

"I think your night's about to get more interesting," she replied, taking a sip of her drink and avoiding my eyes. I turned in the direction she was looking and came face to face with a very frustrated looking Cole.

"Whatever serving I'm on? Seriously, babe?" he demanded.

I shrugged. I actually thought it was a pretty good line. Apparently Cole didn't agree.

"Kat, sorry to break up your ladies night. I brought Sal along, he'll take you home," he ordered firmly.

"We're not done," I protested.

"You are so done," he growled. "Up, or I'll throw you over my shoulder and carry you out of here, I swear to God," he said through his teeth.

I eyed him for a moment and realized that, unfortunately, he would so do that if I pushed him. "Fine," I muttered. "You okay?" I turned to ask Kat.

"Yeah," she said with a smile.

"Maybe you and Sal should stay awhile and have a drink," I suggested with mock innocence.

"Maybe," Kat said as she tried to fight her grin when Sal appeared and took my now vacated spot at the bar.

Maybe some good would come out of this night after all. Cole grasped my hand and led the way authoritatively out of the bar.

"Unless you're taking me home, I'm not getting on that bike," I said firmly when he handed me my helmet. He regarded me with frustration. "I'm serious Cole, I'm not leaving Kat to sleep there alone with all this shit going on," I said forcefully. "And I sure as hell am not going back to that barbecue now," I fumed.

"Christ you are a pain in my ass. Get on," he ordered, turning the ignition. I climbed on behind him not holding him as closely as I normally did and allowed him to take me home.

When we pulled up to the curb, he didn't hesitate in making it perfectly clear that he intended to follow me inside. There was no dissuading him, so I stalked up the stairs and into our place as though he wasn't there. He allowed me this for a few moments as I threw my bag down on the couch and took off my jacket.

"You missed the part where I'd shoved her hand away about a dozen times," he said suddenly, breaking the silence. I turned to face him, arms crossed over my chest. His eyes traveled briefly to the cleavage that the pose created, before his eyes returned to my face. "It's not like I didn't know you were comin'," he pointed out.

I didn't adjust my stance.

"God, I hate fuckin' explaining myself," he muttered before taking a deep breath and blowing it out. "All I meant earlier by Daisy just being Daisy is that she's just one of many. You grew up in a club babe, I know you're not blind to that part of the life," he said, his eyes looking at me a bit anxiously. "But women like Daisy, they have nothing on a woman like you and who you are to me. That's something I'm sure you also know," he said firmly. "You know what it is to be on the back of my bike, in my bed, and at the club. And I like that, a fuck of a lot. I don't have to explain shit to you. You understand my world."

I may understand his world but that didn't mean I would excuse certain behaviors.

"Girls like her, they'll always be there. You gotta deal with that part of it. And you gotta deal with the fact that I have a past. I won't be apologizing for it either," he said firmly. "But I'll admit I could have tried harder to ward her off. I'm just not used to having to. Quite frankly, I barely notice she's there," he said with a shrug.

My stance relaxed only slightly and I was sure he saw it. He took the opportunity to come closer until he was standing right in front of me looking down at me. He took my chin and tilted it up.

"I'm yours too, babe. And I'm glad you want it that way," he said softly. "And if I didn't know I had a fiery red head on my hands before, I certainly do now," he said.

I scowled up at him, but most of the fight had gone out of me.

"I'll give you this and then I'm done," he said quietly. "No one has ever made me feel the way you do. You don't have anything to worry about," he said, his tone nearly pained in its honesty.

I sighed, feeling somewhat relieved, but I still needed to get one thing out in the open. "If I'm sleeping with you, I'm the only one sleeping with you," I emphasized meeting his blue-eyed gaze.

"Wouldn't want it any other way," he said softly, his hand coming up to cup my chin.

His fingers twisted firmly into my hair as he pulled his mouth to mine. He groaned low and deep into my mouth as his hands gripped my ass. I hopped up, twisting my legs around his waist as he held my weight easily and pressed my back into the wall. He pushed himself into me and I could feel his excitement through both of our jeans. I moaned softly, beyond ready to have him inside of me.

"Take me to bed," I demanded, my voice hoarse.

He immediately shifted away from the wall and carried me to my bedroom and threw me on the bed. I'd never been more turned on in my life as he kicked my door shut with his boot.

We were soon tearing at each other's clothes with a

passion I'd never experienced. My teeth raked his neck and my nails found his back as my heels dug into his bare ass trying to push him inside.

"You ready for me already, babe?" he growled.

"God, yes." I breathed.

He sunk all the way into me, making me cry out loudly. It felt so amazing. I allowed him a few thrusts before I rolled us, taking the top and riding him with everything I had.

"Christ, you are so fucking sexy," he groaned, watching me with hooded eyes as I took him. His hands gripped my hips firmly, guiding me as I threw my head back. He moved slightly so he was sitting up and pulled the back of my neck toward him so he could take my mouth in a deep kiss.

"Shit, you're so deep," I whimpered, feeling heat spread over my entire body.

"Tell me your mine," he growled, his eyes locked on mine.

"I'm yours," I answered immediately before I pushed him onto his back, my hand on his chest. "Now, tell me your mine," I repeated his demand with a smile.

He grinned back up at me, "I'm yours, baby," he said while rolling so that he was on top and thrusting hard into me. It was only moments after that with him hitting just the right spot that I cried out as ecstasy washed over me.

Seconds later I heard him groan his release as I continued to shudder around him. He propped himself up on his elbows, still inside of me, and kissed me deeply. His hand came up to tenderly stroke my temple as he looked down at me and I knew in that instant that I loved him.

God, I was so screwed.

"Are you staying?" I asked quietly.

He snorted as though the question was ridiculous. "Yeah, babe."

"I'm absolutely starving, you want something?" I asked quietly as he shifted off of me.

"I could eat," he said with a grin, watching me as I threw on his T-shirt and my pajama shorts.

"What if I was gonna use that?" he asked with a raised brow.

I looked down at the shirt and then back up at him with a slow smile. "Then I'd say you're out of luck," I said and shrugged, squealing as he swatted my ass. He threw his jeans back on and followed me out to the kitchen and sat at the counter as I whipped us up some sandwiches.

"Were you always this feisty?" he asked, trying to suppress a laugh as I handed him his food.

I bit my lip, thinking that over and he burst out laughing. "I'll take that as a yes," he said as he chuckled.

"Well, it depends on who you ask," I answered defensively. "If you could have asked my dad, he would have said yes." I smiled fondly. "But with any guys I dated, then no," I shook my head.

Cole's brows rose incredulously. "So I'm the lucky one then, huh?" he teased.

I blushed furiously and his expression warmed. "What?" he asked gently. "What's with the blushing?"

I shrugged. "I guess with everyone else I just didn't care enough or something," I muttered feeling embarrassed. "I only ever threw attitude around my family or the guys in the club. People who I knew would be around for a while," I gulped, unable to believe I'd just admitted that.

I prepared myself for him to freak out and run as quickly as possible out the front door.

Instead he smiled at me from across the bar. "Well then I really am the lucky one aren't I?" He winked.

God, was he for real?

"What was your dad like?" he asked as I remained across from him, eating my sandwich standing up.

There were so many ways to answer that question I didn't know how to start. "He was strong, loyal, and really fucking strict," I said as I laughed. "Which is probably why I didn't date much. I think the only reason he let Jake near me is that we'd known each other since we were in diapers," I said thoughtfully. "When my mom died he took his position as a solo parent extremely seriously. He was really involved in everything I did. Whenever I had a school play or a ballet recital he and most of the guys from the club would show up." I laughed again. "It was quite a picture, bikers and little ballerinas."

"But I put him through his paces to be sure. I had my own mind from a young age. He would holler at me that I was making him prematurely gray," I continued with a smile. I hadn't talked about my dad in a while, and it felt nice even though it was sad. "He always said at least he'd had plenty of practice because I'd learned from the master, my mother."

"She was a feisty one too, huh?" he asked gently. He'd stopped eating and was watching me with great interest.

"Yeah, I don't remember her well," I swallowed audibly. "Sorry, I don't talk about this stuff much," I apologized for my obvious emotion.

"Don't apologize," he said as he shook his head, his eyes warm with compassion.

I visibly shook it off and continued. "I was just nine when she died. I remember bits and pieces. But mostly

I remember her hair. It was red and wild like mine, and it would fall all around me when she tucked me in," I recalled, unable to stop tears from filling my eyes.

He stood immediately and came around the bar, stopping in front of me and taking me in his arms.

"I just… I had a family, not just my parents, but the club, too," I whispered hoarsely. "I don't think I'll ever get used to the loss of it all," I choked.

"You might not, but you have me," he decreed.

"We've known each other for a very short time Cole," I reminded him.

"You have me," he stated again, pulling me tighter.

I sighed and allowed myself to consider the possibility that it might be true. I didn't have a great history of luck and I wasn't ready to consider that my luck might be changing since I'd met Cole.

After a few moments, I gently pushed him away to collect myself and he went to sit back down, sensing that I needed my space.

"Sal and Kat must be hitting it off," I surmised, changing the subject. It was getting pretty late and I hadn't heard from her.

"Must be," he agreed.

"Is he someone I should be okay with my best friend having a crush on?" I asked.

"Yeah," he replied simply.

"Good," I sighed.

I cleaned up the dishes while he took a call on his cell. I got ready for bed and climbed under the covers listening to his deep voice unable to hear his conversation as he sat in the living room talking.

"Everything okay?" I asked when he came in, as he

divested himself of his jeans and climbed into bed.

"Yeah," he replied, laying on his back with his hand thrown behind his head, appearing deep in thought.

It occurred to me then that I had no idea what his club was into. My dad always ensured that the Sinners stayed clear of drug running and prostitution, but I assumed that had all gone by the wayside with him gone.

"What are the Knights into?" I asked quietly, unsure what type of response he'd give me, if any.

He turned his head toward me and regarded me for a few minutes.

"You don't have to tell me anything, not yet anyway," I assured him when I saw hesitation in his eyes. "And I don't need to know the details. But if I'm gonna have to bail you out of jail anytime soon, I'd like to know what for," I said dryly, earning myself a small smile.

"I don't plan on getting locked up darlin'. But good to know you'd bail me out," he answered, still smiling.

"That's good," I sighed, flopping onto my back.

"We own a couple of bars in town – including the one I took you to the other night, along with some property and a mechanic shop. I take care of the books," he said and shrugged casually.

I tried not to insult him by looking too shocked. "You're good with numbers then?"

"Very. Always have been," he said. "We keep our noses pretty clean, babe," he assured me. "That's not to say there isn't the occasional bullshit and reason to be vigilant, but we can leave it at that for now."

"Okay." I nodded as I looked up at the ceiling. He'd actually told me more than I'd expected.

"You gonna take your pop's place someday?" I asked

curiously.

He shrugged. "Maybe."

I nodded. It wasn't my place to weigh in on such matters, not yet anyway. I left it at that, not wanting to push him.

"We good?" he asked quietly.

"Yeah, we're good." I nodded as he pulled me into his body, wrapping an arm around my shoulder. I felt him kiss my hair and I smiled.

"You set the alarm?" I mumbled, close to drifting off.

"Yeah," he replied before I fell asleep.

Chapter Seven

I woke up abruptly to pounding at the front door.

"What the fuck?" I heard Cole rumble in the darkness as he got up and pulled on his jeans.

I sat up in bed and pulled the covers across my chest. Somewhere in the night I'd gotten hot and taken off his T-shirt.

"Stay there," he ordered before stalking out of my room.

I soon heard heated voices, but I didn't sense any real danger so I threw his T-shirt back on and crept into the living room, curious who was out there.

I was shocked to find Henry, my father's former right hand man in a standoff with Cole.

"Henry?" I asked incredulously.

"Dammit babe, I told you to stay in there," Cole growled.

"What are you doing here?" I asked Henry, ignoring Cole.

"If this asshole would let me in I'd tell you," Henry replied irritably.

"Cole, let him in, it's okay," I said softly. Henry had always been good to me and I believed he'd been loyal to my father. Despite everything that had happened, I trusted him.

He'd always been a large man. He was as tall as Cole but much heavier around the middle than I remembered. Years of beer drinking had finally caught up with him from the looks of it. I was surprised to see that his brown beard now had flecks of gray. They were sprinkled in his long hair as well, which was tied back in his ever-present ponytail. He definitely looked older and a bit tired, and I wondered if the stress of losing my dad accounted for most of that.

Cole swore under his breath and pulled the door open to let Henry in. I went over and gave Henry a hug, feeling nostalgic for one of the few comforts I'd had of home. He embraced me tightly.

"Hi, Rosie," he said, tenderly using the nickname he and my father had always called me.

"Hi Henry," I smiled, feeling tears fill my eyes. "Good to see you," I whispered thickly.

"Wish it was under better circumstances," he muttered as we broke apart.

"And what would those circumstances be?" Cole interrupted, standing behind me, a formidable presence with his arms crossed over his bare chest.

"I came to talk to Rosie. Do us a favor son and give us some privacy," Henry requested.

I winced, knowing Cole wouldn't take too kindly to being called "son." But that was just Henry. He didn't mean anything by it.

"Henry, Cole's my man," I explained. "He takes good care of me. Anything you have to say to me, you can say in front of him," I assured him as I sat on the couch and encouraged Henry to do the same. "I trust him Henry," I emphasized when he still seemed unsure.

He blew out a frustrated breath. "Fine. Didn't think I'd be divulging anything of consequence in front of no Knight, but it's crazy days," he muttered.

I looked at him expectantly ready for him to begin, feeling assured by Cole's presence at my back.

"I know things with the Sinners went to shit a while ago, you had a good sense for that and didn't delay in getting outta there," he began. "I hope you know I was always loyal to your father and to you."

"I do," I said.

"I never knew for sure who killed Ray, but I suspected the same thing we all did. Jake was always a bad apple. Him and that fucking Victor Cross," he swore. "I know you've always watched your back honey, but Jake is on a fucking tear. We voted him out as Prez a while back. He was a fucked up leader, never did the job right. He's somehow convinced that if he can get you back that he'll improve his position. I think that motherfucker has lost his goddamned mind."

I sucked in my breath at this news.

"And I know that he's gotten wind that you've set up with the Knights. He's already made moves against the club," Henry stated, his eyes shifting to Cole's. "The combination honey, it's not good," he said, blowing out a breath.

Cole grasped the back of my neck and squeezed. "He's not going to touch a single fucking hair on your head," he swore.

Henry sighed, looking tired. "Honestly I don't know what he'll do. But I came to warn you. I was worried," he admitted. "All I know is that you need to be careful – as in way fucking careful." Then he turned his eyes to Cole. "The moves being made against the Knights don't speak for my club. I need you to know that. I'd like a meet with your pop," he requested. "Clearly, we've got a few outliers that need to be dealt with," he bit out angrily. "The club as a whole still wants to maintain the partnership we've had for the past twenty years."

"I'll set it up," Cole agreed, his hand on my shoulder.

"I appreciate you looking out for our girl. Something we should have been doing, things just got fucked up," he said, his tone laced with guilt.

Cole simply nodded. "Appreciate the heads up."

Henry rose to stand and I stood with him. "I'll be in town for a few more days, you call me if you need me, okay?" he asked me.

I nodded.

"You're a good girl Rosie, you always were," he said quietly, his expression tender and fatherly. "I want you safe."

"I will be," I assured him, though I wasn't at all sure if that was true.

"It's taken care of," Cole assured him. "I'll be in touch," he added.

Henry nodded and headed for the door with a parting flick of the wrist. A gesture I hadn't seen in eight years. It was so simple, and yet, it made my heart clench.

I stood silently for a few moments after he shut the door behind him, a bit shocked and overwhelmed.

"Babe," Cole said gently after a few minutes.

"Hmm?" I asked absently.

"Come on, let's go to bed," he coaxed, holding a hand

out to me. I took it without thought and followed him to my room. He tucked me in and soon joined me, pulling me into his side "It's gonna be okay," he said softly.

I didn't reply. I had nothing to say. He didn't know that, he couldn't.

I woke up earlier than I would have liked and heard Cole's deep voice on the phone out in the living room. I looked at my phone to make sure Kat had texted me back. She'd never come home and I had reached out to make sure she was okay. Sure enough, there was a text saying she'd stayed with Sal. There was definitely a story to be told there and I was looking forward to the distraction.

I lay in bed trying to collect myself for a few minutes when Cole returned, already showered and dressed. He leaned over me with a hand on either side of me, kissing me soundly. He smelled like soap and Cole. I breathed him in.

"I gotta go babe, shit to do," he explained.

"Okay, I'll call you after work," I said sleepily.

His brow wrinkled for a moment and something flashed in his eyes before he sighed. "Call your boss and take some time off," he directed in that bossy way of his that drove me crazy.

"What? No," I said as I shook my head, suddenly more awake.

"Were you not here last night?" he demanded. "Until this fucker is dealt with you're not going to give him an invitation to get near you," he said, his voice low and intense.

"Well, I couldn't be around many more people than when I'm at work," I retorted. We stared at each other for a few minutes and I softened when I saw how worried he was. "I have bills to pay, honey," I explained. "I'm not going to hide away for God knows how long. I promise to be careful, but I still have to live my life," I said, putting a hand on his cheek and grazing it gently down to his neck where I could feel his pulse. "I'm going to go to the gym, too. I'll go stir crazy otherwise," I explained.

"If I can't take you home, promise me you'll wait until somebody from the club collects you," he ordered. "From anywhere you go," he added.

I was tempted to quip that I really couldn't picture Wes or Sal jogging next to me on a treadmill, but I decided to bite my tongue.

"Cole!" I protested.

"No, darlin'." He shook his head. "Even that's less than I'm comfortable with. You agree to that or you get chained to the bed."

Something about those words sent an unexpected thrill through me. "Chained to the bed?" I smiled seductively. "That sounds fun," I said, biting my lower lip.

His eyes dilated in response and he groaned. "Shit, I really have to go. Otherwise, I'd stay and play, baby."

"Damn," I muttered.

He leaned in and kissed me, closed mouth. If he let it become more we both knew he'd never leave. And with that, he shoved off the bed and stalked from the room. I heard him set the alarm and soon after his bike roared off.

Kat came home as I was finishing up in the shower.

"Spill!" I exclaimed after I'd thrown some clothes on and she was flopped on my bed.

"Oh God, Scar, I am in trouble," she groaned.

I laughed, knowing the feeling all too well.

"I take it you had fun?" I asked and cocked a brow at

her.

"He's so fucking hot," she sighed. "I didn't plan on spending the night at his place, but Cole called and said it probably wasn't a good idea for me to come home. Which I want to hear about, by the way," she noted.

"Later," I said dismissively. I was so tired of my shit. I wanted to talk about someone else. "So what happened?"

"We stayed at the bar for another drink and we just hit it off," she sighed dreamily. "Then after he talked to Cole he took me to his place and we watched movies and made out," she said as she giggled.

I smiled, happy for her.

"He was a perfect gentleman, until I forced him not to be," she said.

"Good for you," I said.

"He is amazing in bed, Scar. Like A-MA-zing," she emphasized.

I nodded, knowing all too well what she meant.

"He's having a thing at his house tonight. You're coming," she said, pointing a finger at me.

"I'll see if the warden will allow it," I muttered.

"What's going on?" she asked.

I sighed and gave her a brief recap of Henry's visit.

"God, Cole must want to kill that bastard," she said when I was done.

"He's not pleased," I agreed.

"What about you, how are you?" she asked, concerned.

"I've been better," I admitted. "All the more reason for you to distract me with Sal stories and for us to go have some fun tonight," I said as I grinned, lightening the mood.

"Sounds good to me," she said as she smiled. Then she reached over and grasped my hand. "I like this new

Scarlet."

I had to admit despite all the rest of the bullshit, I did too.

Kat joined me at the gym and we had a good workout. Wes picked us up without muttering a word of complaint, despite both Kat and I feeling a bit awkward about it. I'd been getting to know Connie even better over the last few weeks and I had begun to consider her a good friend. It felt odd to have my friend's boyfriend playing bodyguard. He basically told us to can it after we thanked him for the ride the third time.

I fired off a text to Cole before I headed to work. He said he'd pick me up after work and we'd head to Sal's together. I was looking forward to it.

Connie and I got ready in the bathroom together after work, laughing and gossiping. I decided to walk on the wild side a bit and wear fairly short black shorts, a very tight fitting and low cut tank top, and my kick ass ankle boots. I dressed it up a bit with a chunky necklace and tamed my hair into a French braid of sorts that I was wearing over my shoulder. Wes was picking Connie up and we were all meeting Kat there. When we emerged, Cole and Wes were posted at the bar with beers.

"We thought you might be a while," Cole surmised correctly as I ducked under his arm and kissed his neck.

"Good thinking," I said as I smiled against his neck.

"You look hot," he whispered in my ear.

I grinned, pleased.

"You about ready?" he wanted to know.

I nodded and we headed out. There was something so thrilling about roaring off on the back of Cole's bike with Wes and Connie behind us. In that moment I felt so strongly that I belonged right where I was, something I hadn't felt in my entire life. I squeezed Cole's torso in a silent thank you for being such a large part of creating that feeling for me.

Sal lived in a little bungalow not far from Cole's. I saw quite a few bikes parked out front as we pulled up behind Kat's Corolla. Cole grasped my hand and led me inside, lifting his chin to almost everyone we passed through the crowded house filled with music. The house was so full I could barely take in what the place was like, aside from the fact that it was sparse. He grabbed us beers from the fridge and led us outside to a folding chair where he promptly pulled me into his lap.

I laughed at his possessive hold. "Well, ok then," I said and grinned, looking down and kissing him.

He gave me a crooked grin in return and squeezed my neck in that gesture I had come to love.

The backyard was plain. It had a large concrete patio and some simple landscaping bordering it. The whole yard was enclosed by a high fence that provided a sense of privacy, but it obviously did nothing for the noise of the rowdy crowd. I assumed that if he had these get-togethers often, either his neighbors hated him or they had some sort of understanding.

A cute brunette with curly hair approached almost immediately. If it weren't for her welcoming smile I'd worry that she was one of Cole's past flings.

"Hi, Scarlet, I'm Ettie," she said and grinned.

I gasped and smiled back. "So you do exist," I said as I laughed.

"So how much credit should I take for you two getting together?" she teased Cole. I liked her immediately.

Cole chuckled as a tall, heavy set guy with a buzz cut came out to join us.

"I'm Mack, Ettie's man," he introduced, holding out a hand.

"Nice to meet you," I said and shook his hand as I marveled that such a petite woman seemed to fit so well with this huge man. But they clearly adored each other. It was apparent within two minutes of seeing them together. Mack promptly put an arm around his girl and kissed her temple sweetly.

"Need a beer darlin'?" he asked.

"I'm good for now," she said as she smiled, her eyes alight.

"How long have you two been together?" I asked as the guys started talking shop.

"Five years," she told me.

"Wow with how smitten you two seem, I would think it would have been mere months," I said with a laugh.

"We're lucky," she said. "Though I'll tell you, all these guys, they get a girl and that's it, or so it would seem," she added.

I tilted my head, beyond interested in what she was saying.

"They play the field and fuck anything that walks, but once they settle, they settle," she said with a wink.

"Has Cole, um... settled before to your knowledge?" I asked.

She shook her head. "You're the talk of the town," she replied.

I wasn't quite sure how to feel about that. Cole pulled me back down on his lap and I focused on finishing my beer instead.

"Scar, there you are!" Kat exclaimed, finding us outside. "Can I steal her for a bit Cole?" she asked.

He nodded, "I suppose. Don't get into any trouble," he said, kissing me solidly.

"Wouldn't dream of it," I said, winking at him.

Kat took my hand and led me back into the house where we got another beer.

"What's up?" I asked.

"Sal is being weird," she muttered.

"Weird?" I asked as she pulled me to the relatively empty living room and onto the couch.

"Standoffish," she sighed.

I'd been afraid of that and knew she had been too.

"Oh sweetie, I'm sorry," I said sympathetically.

"Ugh, I shouldn't have slept with him so soon," she groaned. "I never do that, but I couldn't seem to help it!" she lamented.

"You went with your instincts and you had fun, right?"
She nodded.

"He might come around. For now I'd just give him his space, make him come to you. If he knows what's good for him, he will," I said firmly.

"What's going on ladies?" Connie asked, plopping on the couch next to us.

Kat took a moment to fill her in.

Connie waved her hand dismissively. "Sal's just weird like that. I wouldn't read much into it."

"Yeah well I'm not into being treated like a pariah after I sleep with a guy," Kat muttered.

"I hear you," Connie agreed. "Wes was a bit like that at first," she confided. I found that hard to believe with how much he clearly doted on her now. "I think some of these tough guys are just like that at first when they meet a woman they actually like. They don't know what to do with it after all the skanks they're used to," she said dryly. "But Sal is a mystery to all of us to begin with. He's so guarded it's hard to get to know him even a little bit. Just play a little hard to get, see what happens," she advised.

"Done and done. I don't even have to play," Kat muttered.

I squeezed her thigh for a moment in reassurance, hoping like hell that Sal pulled his head out of his ass. Kat was gorgeous and funny and just amazing all around. She deserved the best. She also had a temper that you did not want to fuck around with.

I went to find the bathroom and then planned to look for Cole. The house was small, but I meandered a bit trying to find it. I was slightly tipsy and the house was packed.

"Looking for something sweet cheeks?" a deep voice inquired. I turned to find a very handsome dark haired man looking hungrily at my ass.

"Did you seriously just call me 'sweet cheeks?'" I asked, dumbfounded that he had the nerve.

"Well, it's a seriously sweet ass," he said, moving toward me.

"You don't back up immediately, we have a serious fucking problem Parker," Cole's voice boomed from behind me.

"Oh sorry man. This yours?" my asshole admirer said as he nodded toward me, immediately backing up.

"Is this yours?" I repeated back his words with supreme irritation. "Seriously? Are you fucking kidding me?" I demanded incredulously.

"Baby, cool it," Cole commanded, putting a hand on

my waist.

Oh no, I did not think so. I would not be told to "cool it" but I knew enough to have those words later, not in front of an audience.

I turned back to Jerk Face. "A word of advice: you ever want to raise your standards a bit and try getting a decent piece of tail, I wouldn't start off by calling a woman 'sweet cheeks,'" I advised.

I felt Cole stiffen behind me. Clearly he hadn't heard that part.

"I also wouldn't refer to a woman akin to an inanimate object," I added helpfully.

The guy chuckled and turned amused eyes to Cole. "Got your hands full, huh Jackson?" he taunted. His quip clearly had a double meaning as he took a good long look at my breasts and backside.

I narrowed my eyes.

"You want to make this an issue, you keep talkin'," Cole goaded, his voice full of menace.

Oh dear, perhaps it was time to try to diffuse the situation.

"Forget it babe, let's go get a beer," I prompted, even though my bladder was now seriously protesting.

But Cole didn't even spare me a glance. He was too busy glaring at Parker.

"Babe," I prompted, quietly putting a hand on his chest.

"What the fuck are you doing here?" Sal demanded of Parker, coming to join our tense little huddle. "You weren't invited. Get the fuck out."

"Just came to see how the other half lives," Parker replied as he chuckled. "Clearly, the other half is pussy whipped," he said with a grin. "Though, I admit, I can't say I blame you man." He winked at Cole.

"One more word and you won't be able to fucking walk tomorrow," Cole threatened.

Parker held up his hands in surrender, though he was still visibly amused as he walked away.

"Who was that?" I demanded.

"One of the reasons to remain vigilant," Cole muttered unhelpfully. "Let's go get that beer."

"Actually, you go. The whole reason I came in here was to pee. Where's the bathroom?" I asked him.

He pointed me in the right direction, still seeming aggravated. Perhaps leaving him alone for a few minutes wasn't a bad idea anyway. It was clear that he and that Parker guy had some sort of history and it wasn't a good one.

When I found the bathroom it was locked, so I leaned against the wall patiently waiting for it to become unoccupied.

I groaned inwardly when I heard obvious retching from the bathroom. I debated for a moment on what to do before I knocked quietly.

"Hey, can I get you something?" I offered. "Water?"

"Water, please," a female voice croaked a response.

Moments later I returned with a huge plastic cup filled with water and knocked again. I was taken aback slightly when my not so favorite person, Daisy, opened the door. But she looked so sick I couldn't hold a grudge.

"Here you go," I offered.

"Thanks," she muttered, mascara running down her face.

"Here, I've got some makeup remover wipes in my

purse," I offered, entering the decent sized bathroom and closing the door behind me. The smell of vomit was strong, and I cracked the window after handing her a wipe.

"Should have had dinner," she muttered.

"Been there," I replied sympathetically.

"You're Cole's new woman, huh?" she asked.

I nodded a bit wearily.

"I would have really preferred to dislike you," she muttered.

I laughed despite myself as she wiped up her makeup into some semblance of normalcy.

"Us girls gotta stick together don't you think?" I said and smiled, cocking my head at her in the mirror.

"Not a stance I'm used to, but I like it," she muttered.

"Mind if I pee since I'm already in here?" I asked, thankful the toilet had a separate door.

"Go ahead," she replied, looking herself over in the mirror.

I peed, washed my hands, and regarded her for a moment in the mirror. "Much better," I said. "I'll let you finish up." I opened the door to leave and give her some privacy.

"Hey, um… thanks," she called to me.

"Sure thing," I replied and almost ran into Cole on the way out.

"I was looking for you," he said, looking quizzically at me. "Who was in the bathroom?"

"Oh, Daisy had a little too much to drink. I just got her some water and some makeup remover," I said as I shrugged nonchalantly. "I could use that beer now," I added as he followed me out to the kitchen.

"You were in there helpin' Daisy?" he asked, clearly

confused.

I sighed, exasperated. "Yeah babe, of course. It's not like I hate her or anything. She wasn't being vindictive the other night. She was just playing the role she knows," I said. "I doubt she knew you were spoken for. From what I gather the knowledge is slightly surprising to folks," I said dryly. "If she had her hands all over you now that we're clear, that'd be a different story," I clarified.

"Uh huh," he replied, still regarding me as though I'd grown two heads.

I rolled my eyes at him as he took my hand and led me back outside. It was clear that he didn't intend to let me out of his sight for the rest of the night, which was fine by me. I sat perched on his lap and laughed with Connie, Ettie, and some of the guys. It felt very natural spending time with all of them and I couldn't remember the last time I'd had such a fun, carefree night despite our earlier run in with Parker.

When Kat emerged from the house a while later, I locked eyes with her to carefully assess her mood. She met my gaze and I knew I needed to take care of my friend.

"Babe, I'm gonna go home with Kat," I told Cole quietly in his ear, still perched on his knee.

"What?" he asked.

"She's not having a good night," I explained, not wanting to go into the details. "We look out for each other. As much fun as I'm having and as much as I'd love to stay, I gotta take care of my girl," I said, kissing him when he turned his face to look up into mine.

"Take her to my place," he instructed. "I'll stay here a while longer, give you time to talk with your girl. But then I end the day with you in my bed," his deep voice rumbled in my ear. "Put her up in the guest room."

"You sure?" I asked, surprised and pleased by the suggestion.

He nodded. "Hank is trailing you to my place," he added, referring to one of the many new Knights I'd met that evening.

"It's a few blocks," I protested.

He leveled me with a look and I sighed. "Okay, fine," I relented before I kissed him again and arose from his lap. I did need to be careful these days.

I headed straight for Kat, took her hand, and led her out of the house without a word. Once we were on the street, I put an arm around her and started walking. I knew Hank was behind us, but he kept his distance and it almost felt like we were alone.

"We're going to Cole's," I explained. "He has a guest room and he'll give us some time."

"Okay," she mumbled, and my heart broke for how crestfallen she seemed.

We walked silently for a while as I let her collect her thoughts. "What happened?" I asked finally.

"Nothing new since I talked to you earlier – he basically didn't acknowledge me all night," she sighed, and I could hear the quaver in her voice. "It was so embarrassing," she groaned. "I feel like such an idiot! I thought with how great the other night was and with him inviting me tonight that something was happening between us. God, I sound like such a cliché," she groaned again.

"You're not an idiot or a cliché, sweetie," I assured her as we neared Cole's place. "I would have thought the same thing. It sounds like maybe he's just a bit clueless and closed off," I added.

"I just felt so exposed all night, vulnerable. And you

know how I hate that."

"I do," I agreed, using the key Cole had given me to let us into his place. I waved briefly to Hank to let him know we were okay.

"Nice place," she said distractedly as we put our purses down.

I grabbed us two beers from the fridge and we sat on the couch. "Yeah," I agreed, looking around in appreciation. He clearly took care of his home, kept it neat for a bachelor.

"So what are you going to do?" I asked her quietly as she slouched on the couch and put her feet up on the coffee table.

"Nothing to be done except to assume that I was just another one-night stand and that I won't hear from him again. I'll be damned if I'm gonna reach out to him," she said with a grimace.

"Good for you."

"I just really liked him, you know?" she practically whispered. "I know you warned me, but I haven't felt that excited about a guy in a long time. He was different than what I usually go for, but I liked it. I liked him."

"I know," I replied sympathetically as her phone dinged.

"What the fuck?" she asked, her brows knitted when she looked at the text and then showed it to me.

"Where'd you go?" It read from Sal.

I couldn't help but laugh, but I bit my lip when she glared at me. "Clearly clueless sweetie," I laughed again.

"God, is he serious?" she exclaimed. "I was at his house for four hours. He barely talked to me, but then twenty minutes after I leave, he wants to know where I went! He's probably just bummed he's not getting any tonight," she glowered.

"Maybe, maybe not." I shrugged. "How are you going to play it?" I wondered, genuinely curious.

She bit her lip, thinking for a minute before typing out a response and showing it to me.

"A four hour brush off was more than enough for me. Have a good one."

I smiled. Kat and I certainly didn't lack in the feisty department.

"Well, at least you know he noticed where you were even if he wasn't talking to you," I offered, trying not to laugh.

She snorted. "Well, he'll have to do a hell of a lot better than that."

"For sure," I agreed readily.

We sat drinking our beers and chatting for a while. Kat's mood had lightened some with the knowledge that he at least cared that she'd left, and we giggled and talked as we always did.

We heard the rumble of bikes not an hour later. "Hmm, that's more than one bike," I mused.

Kat's eyes widened in shock and we looked at each other, listening.

"Maybe he pulled his head out of his ass," I said as I laughed.

Sure enough, Cole and Sal walked through the door seconds later. I took a moment to study Sal. I wondered what in his history made him so aloof with women. I couldn't help but notice again how handsome he was. I was glad to see that he only had eyes for my girl as he walked into the room.

"Let's talk outside," he rumbled at Kat. Obviously

bossiness ran rampant in this club.

"Fine," she huffed with irritation. She was gonna make him work for it for sure. She followed him out front and I bit my lip to stop from smiling.

"What's goin' on there?" Cole asked gruffly, sitting down next to me and hauling me into his lap to kiss my neck.

"He's gonna have to step it up if he likes her," I replied with a shrug.

"Sal's not used to havin' to work for it," he replied immediately.

"Well, neither are you," I pointed out with a small smile.

"Point taken," he muttered, making me laugh outright.

"Seen you laugh so much tonight," he observed, his expression soft as he regarded me.

"I'm happy." I shrugged.

"Glad to hear it," he replied quietly.

"I feel like, when I'm with you that I have a place in any given moment – wherever we are," I admitted softly, hoping I wouldn't freak him out. "Thank you for that," I said.

His eyes flared as his grip around my waist tightened and I saw raw emotion flash across his face.

I leaned in and kissed him passionately, unable to contain myself, despite the risk that Sal and Kat could walk back in at any moment.

"Bed," Cole said gruffly, standing with me still in his lap and beginning to carry me out of the room.

"But Sal and Kat…" I protested.

"They'll figure it out," he cut me off.

I giggled helplessly at his exuberance as he threw me

on the bed and kicked the door shut.

"Oh God, Cole," I breathed sometime later as he pounded into me, his mouth at my neck. I could barely feel my limbs as I clung to him. He bit my shoulder gently and it was enough to hurl me over the edge, with him following shortly thereafter.

"Fuck," he groaned, his voice deep and strained as he put some of his weight on me. I loved the feeling of his strong body over mine and I squeezed him tighter still. I was so tempted to let the words slip that I knew to be true, but I held them in.

"They're gone, right?" I asked quietly after a few moments.

Cole burst out laughing and rolled off of me. "Yeah babe, you didn't hear Sal's bike?"

"I don't think I would have heard a marching band," I muttered. He continued to chuckle and pulled me to his chest as he lay on his back, still breathing hard.

"My pop agreed to meet with Henry tomorrow," he informed me after we'd been quiet for a while. His fingers stroked through my long hair leisurely.

"Good," I replied simply. "Despite everything, I still trust Henry and it would seem that I have a good sense for these things," I added.

"So it would seem," he agreed, kissing my head briefly.

"What was that situation with that Parker guy tonight?" I asked curiously.

He sighed. "Allen Parker. The guy is a worm. He used to hang around more, we even thought at one point that he'd become a prospect. But he screwed Axel's girl at the time... big mistake. Then he tried to skim off the top of one of the projects we gave him. He hasn't been welcome since then," he stated.

"Yeah but why do you have such an issue with him?" I pressed, knowing that wasn't the whole story.

"I'm just pissed that I was a poor judge of character. I liked the guy, trusted him even. My pop had my balls for vouching for him," he grumbled.

"Ah," I nodded, finally understanding. All of the Sinners had always prided themselves on being able to judge character. Trust was a huge variable. If you were wrong about it, or about someone, you could be seriously fucked. "It's happened to all of us," I said and shrugged, hoping he'd brush it off.

"Yeah," he agreed. I could tell he was deep in thought.

I left him to it and got up to get ready for bed, padding over to the bathroom. I'd packed a few overnight essentials just in case, and I was grateful to be able to wash my face and brush my teeth.

After I crawled back in bed with Cole, he pulled my back to his front, he wrapped his arm around my waist, and we both fell asleep.

Chapter Eight

Cole surprised me the next morning by asking me to come to the club with him after we finished breakfast. "I want to keep you close," he said simply when I asked why.

"Okay," I agreed, grateful that I brought a change of clothes with me.

We hopped on his bike and I was surprised at how many of the guys were there, including Sal. I was thrilled when I saw Kat, too.

I hugged her. "It's a big deal he brought you here, you know," I whispered in her ear.

"I know," she replied.

"You okay to hang out while we meet?" Cole wanted to know.

"Yeah, we'll catch some rays," I said as I smiled at him. He leaned down to kiss me tenderly. God, he was awesome. I couldn't believe my badass biker was willing to be openly affectionate with me in front of his guys. My stereotypes definitely didn't apply to him, in most ways anyway.

Kat and I got comfortable on the chairs out front where there was more sun, and sunned ourselves as the guys took care of business inside.

"So tell me everything," I demanded, my face upturned to the sun as I sighed in contentment. It was a beautiful day and I was in love. Couldn't get much better than that.

"He apologized," she said. "Sincerely," she added when I looked over at her. "I don't think he realized what an ass he was being."

"Told you." I grinned.

"He's got some work to do, but I think he likes me, at least enough to apologize, which I have the feeling he's not used to doing," she said with a smirk.

"Definitely not," I said, as a black SUV with tinted windows came screeching to a halt at the curb.

"Let's go inside," I said immediately as the hair rose at the back of my neck. "Go!" I shouted more desperately when I saw Jake and two other men jump out of the car and race toward us.

We were up and running for the doors of the club when a strong arm wrapped around me and I saw Victor-Fucking-Cross grab Kat.

"No, not her!" I screamed angrily as they dragged us quickly to the SUV. I couldn't believe they had the balls to snatch us in front of the Knights' headquarters. Clearly they were sending a message.

"Cole!" I screamed as loud as I could as I kicked and struggled with everything I was worth. I was shoved into the back seat with Kat. I saw Cole and the rest of the guys come hurtling out of the doors, murder in their faces as we tore off from the curb.

"Why the fuck did you take her?" Jake demanded gesturing to Kat, his eyes blazing as the SUV swerved through traffic. I didn't recognize the driver. It had been eight years since I'd set eyes on Jake and the years had not been kind. His dark, wavy hair was now shaved close to his head, making his already hollow face look more so. His dark brown eyes looked wild, and they were framed by dark circles as he glanced around the truck with a hysteria that I'd never seen him exhibit. He was either on something or was just that deranged. There was nothing left of the Jake I remembered from my youth, though that fact had already been confirmed during our last encounter.

"I don't know, she was just there so I grabbed her," Victor replied as both men tried to subdue us. Neither Kat nor I were making that easy, as I bit down hard on Jake's forearm.

"Motherfucking bitch!" he bellowed, punching me hard in the face. Kat screamed.

Damn, that hurt. Especially with that fucking ring he was wearing. I saw stars briefly, but it only served to piss me off more. "Do you have a fucking death wish?" I screeched.

"Not as much as you do," Jake sneered. "Now calm the fuck down," he barked.

"Let Kat go, she has no part in this," I demanded.

"She does now," he answered sharply.

Fuck.

I heard the roar of Harleys behind us and realized that Jake really had lost his mind. How had he figured he'd snatch us without swift and violent retribution? I hadn't known Cole long, but I knew Jake would be lucky to escape with his life after this stunt. You did not fuck with another man's woman, especially on his turf.

"You tell your new boy toy that this is only a taste of what I'm going to do," Jake demanded, pulling my already bruised face close to his. "You tell him they better start giving me some goddamn respect," he added before he kissed me roughly on the mouth. I fought back the urge to gag. "Missed you babe, look forward to having you back where you belong," he said with a cruel smile. "But until then…" he trailed off as the door was swung open.

My heart raced as I realized his intention – what his intention had been all along. This was simply a stunt designed to scare me and fuck with the Knights, and it was one that Kat and I would pay for with blood. "Don't toss 'em too hard, Vic. I need her in one piece," Jake called casually as Vic made a grab for Kat and hauled her out of the SUV to the pavement. I heard her scream and bit back a sob, caring far less what happened to me. Kat was just an innocent bystander in this mess.

"I hate your fucking guts," I seethed while looking at Jake straight on.

"We'll see," he said, watching as I met the same fate as my best friend.

Pain seared over the exposed skin of my legs and arms as the pavement came cruelly up to meet me. It sliced through my hip and side as I came skidding to a painful halt. The SUV had slowed some as we were tossed out, but not enough to prevent injury. I heard a screech of tires and voices shouting as I tried to ascertain if I was still in one piece.

"Motherfucker!" I heard Cole roar as he came crashing to my side.

"Kat?" I asked desperately.

"She's okay," he bit out, looking down at me with an expression so angry I could barely see the blue of his eyes.

"Where else are you hurt?" he demanded, his eyes taking a quick survey of my body. "Is anything broken?"

"I'm not sure," I answered honestly. "Just give me a second." I breathed, lying on my back looking up at the sky. My whole body throbbed, it was impossible to tell what kind of state I was really in.

"Where's Kat?" I asked after her again.

"She's sitting up, Sal's with her. She's okay baby," he soothed, his voice gruff with emotion.

I nodded as tears welled up in my eyes. "It's my fault," I said hoarsely, feeling so insanely guilty for what had happened to her.

"Baby, this shit is not your fault," he said angrily. "Put that out of your head and let's focus on getting you up off the road okay?" he asked.

I nodded, glancing around. We were out in the middle of nowhere. Jake's SUV had quickly and purposefully headed directly out of town, not hard to do since the club was already on the outskirts.

"Do you need an ambulance?" he asked, his voice tight with worry.

"I don't think so," I said as I shook my head. I took a deep breath and made an effort to sit up. Cole brought his hand to the back of my head helping me carefully. I sat up looking around dazedly until I located Kat, sitting not fifteen feet away. Sal was hunched over her but she looked okay. I sighed in relief.

"Pop's bringin' the truck, then we're going to the hospital," Cole said firmly.

"I think I'm okay," I argued.

"Baby, I don't want to freak you out, but you're in shock. Trust me we need to go to the hospital," he answered firmly.

I squinted up to look at him, the sun streaming behind

his emotion-stricken face. "Okay," I agreed quietly.

We were soon surrounded by Harley's and Cal's SUV.

"Come on, baby," Cole coaxed, picking me up off the ground and carrying me carefully in his arms to the back seat. Sal was depositing Kat gently in on the other side.

"Shit, we're back in another SUV," I groaned over to Kat. And despite ourselves, we both burst out laughing. Maybe we were both just completely hysterical, or maybe it was just really funny. Cole looked at me like I had completely lost it before he shut the door.

"That motherfucker is dead, do you hear me?" I heard him demand of his father. The words were muffled through the door, but there was no mistaking his rage.

"Not disputin' that shit, son, but you need to lock yourself down," Cal ordered.

"Did you see her?" Cole roared. "Did you fucking see her face?"

I winced at the raw emotion in his voice.

"I said, lock that shit down. Come here," Cal commanded, pulling Cole out of hearing distance.

Kat and I regarded each other for a moment.

"If you even think of saying you're sorry I'll blacken your other eye," she warned tersely as Sal hopped up into the passenger side. "This isn't your fault," she reached a hand over to mine, squeezing gently. "Love you, Scar."

I simply nodded, swallowing back my tears, unable to speak, and laid my head back and closed my eyes. The pain was getting worse now that the shock was wearing off. My skin felt like it had been torn off in certain places and my face and joints throbbed.

Cole returned quickly and hopped into the driver's seat, peeling out and gunning it for the hospital.

"What's the story?" I asked hoarsely.

"Story?" Cole asked, peering at me through the rearview mirror. Even in my state I had to admire the color of his eyes as they locked with mine.

"Well, I assume telling the hospital that a rival motorcycle club kidnapped us and threw us from a moving vehicle is out," I replied dryly.

"Right, that story," Cole muttered.

"We'll just tell them we were fucking around trying to learn how to ride motorcycles and ditched them," Kat answered, her voice weak with pain.

Sal twisted in his seat to look at her, his face full of concern, "What about her face?" he asked, turning to look at me briefly before his eyes found Kat again.

"Best to stick with one story," I said, my own voice growing more and more quiet. "They won't push too hard." I sighed.

"How do you know so much about this?" Cole barked at me. He clearly had a fairly loose hold on himself.

"You have got to chill, Bud," Sal said quietly but firmly.

The lump rose again in my throat at what my past was doing to the people dearest to me. Cole was clearly torn up inside while Kat was quite literally torn up. I gazed out the window thinking about how much easier it would be if I just removed myself from both of their lives. I was confident that with me out of the picture, any twisted interest Jake had taken would fall to the wayside.

Cole nodded briefly, his jaw set tightly and the rest of the short drive was silent.

Both Sal and Cole carried us into the emergency room while barking orders at the staff. Words were exchanged, but I was in too much pain and too overwhelmed by the day to pay attention. Everything went relatively smoothly until the nurses asked Cole to leave the room.

"I'm not leavin'," he scowled with his feet planted firmly, arms crossed over his formidable chest.

"Baby, it's okay," I assured him. "I'm sure these nice women are just doing their jobs," I said quietly from the bed they placed me in. I knew they just wanted to question me in private about my story, something I was sure from Cole's expression that he knew as well. I also felt it prudent that he didn't witness the extent of my injuries, at least not at the moment, when he clearly didn't have a handle on his anger. He was still visibly seething, which wasn't helping the nurses to believe my story.

"Fine, ten minutes. No more," he said firmly before turning on his heel and stalking off.

The nurse turned to me, concern in her eyes as she began to gingerly remove my clothing with scissors. They already gave me something for the pain and I focused on the ceiling, not wanting to see the extent of my injuries.

"Are you safe at home?" she asked quietly when she had me situated with a gown covering my naked body. "You can tell me, I swear it won't get back to him," she added. Her eyes brimmed with sincerity, and I knew had the situation called for it that I would have trusted her.

I turned to her with a small smile. "I promise I am. I was just reckless and he worries about me," I assured her. "I have no doubt I'd be safe to confide in you, but there's no need." I smiled and gave her hand a small squeeze. She studied me for a moment before nodding briefly. I couldn't tell if she believed me or not. If I was her I probably wouldn't given the circumstances.

After that, Cole never left my side. He kept a forced

lid on his anger when the doctor discussed how to care for the terrible road rash that I sustained on my left side, but he didn't lose it. I knew he wanted to, but he didn't. Even after everything Jake had done to me, I still couldn't believe that the boy I'd lost my virginity to was capable of such violence against me. He had no compassion, no remorse, and no soul. It was true that I was never in love with him, but I certainly felt something for him – we'd known each other our entire lives. And now I was just a vessel of vengeance in his sick mind. He wanted to hurt me badly, but even worse, he wanted to hurt the people I cared about. I was grateful when they got me into a hospital bed, administering pain medication that quickly knocked me out. I needed a mental and physical break from it all.

Chapter Nine

I was awoken from an incessant beeping, and for a brief moment I thought it was my alarm clock. Then it all came rushing back that I was in the hospital.

"Cole," I murmured, my voice sounding hoarse.

"Right here, baby," his soft voice sounded in my ear.

"Do you realize this is only like our third date?" I mumbled.

"Wouldn't classify this as a date darlin'," his deep voice replied, and I felt his hand stroke my hair back from my forehead.

"Bet you miss the days of, what's her name again?" I searched my muddled mind for her name. "Daisy, that's it. Daisy," I continued to mumble. "So much easier with a girl like her," I said as I began to drift off.

"Didn't cross my mind for a second, sweetheart. Nowhere else I'd rather be," he assured me.

I made a scoffing sound and drifted back to sleep.

When I woke up a second time, I was more lucid. It was very dark in the room and I assumed it was the middle of the night. I took a moment to take in my surroundings. Cole was asleep, his large form slumped over in the chair by the window. My heart immediately lurched that this man who'd known me for such a short period of time was so clearly devoted to me. I had so few people to depend on, so few people that I could trust in the last eight years. Before my father died, he was always at my back, ready to protect me. And before things went south, I had the club. I'd known those men and their families since I was a little girl. After losing everything I had to keep myself closely guarded, the only person I truly let in was Kat. But now this man was knocking away at all my armor after just a few weeks. I was already hopelessly in love with him, something I'd never experienced in my life. I couldn't stand the thought of him getting hurt, of him losing anyone close to him because of me. He already suffered because of my history. I felt tears prick the back of my eyes as I realized that the very best thing I could do for him was let him go.

When I woke up again, sunlight was streaming in through the windows. The chair that Cole had occupied the night before was empty. I sat up, assessing my pain level. My joints were sore, especially my wrists – I had been lucky to avoid a break. My left side was incredibly tender, but I could manage with the help of some pain medication.

A new morning shift nurse came in to take my blood pressure. "Do you know where my boyfriend went?" I asked her, the term sounding silly when spoken aloud. Cole was far more than a boy and the term seemed so... casual.

"He wanted me to tell you that he went to meet with his father for a short while. He was reluctant to leave you," she said as she smiled. "Quite a looker that one," she added.

"I know," I sighed, my throat feeling tight with what I planned to do.

She finished taking my vitals and left me to the quiet

of my hospital room. I realized that if I didn't go now, I'd never have the gumption to do it at all. The thought of not being with Cole felt like being thrown from the SUV all over again – except this time there would be scars.

I swung myself out of the bed and quickly dressed in the clean clothes someone had brought me. Whoever it had been, they thoughtfully brought me a dress so there would be minimal rubbing against my sore and bandaged side. I didn't know how much time I had before he got back, and I knew if I had one look at him I'd lose my nerve. I didn't know where I was going or what I'd do, but the fierce desire to protect him and to protect Kat was all I could think about. I knew I was making myself vulnerable by heading out on my own, but I'd done it successfully before and I could do it again.

I asked a nurse for Kat's room number, and after peering inside to make sure the coast was clear, I quietly opened her door. She was propped up watching TV, looking small and pale in her bed. My eyes welled up at the sight.

"Hi," I said softly when she looked over at me in surprise.

"Hi, are they discharging you already?" she asked with raised brows seeing me fully clothed. She muted the television and turned her knowing blue eyes to me.

I simply looked at her with tears in my eyes and shook my head.

"Scarlet, what the hell?" she demanded, immediately understanding my expression. "We've been over this. Don't you dare do something stupid!"

"I'm sorry, Kat. I love you so much, you've been my family. You've been everything to me, and I can't stand what my past has done to you, or could do to you," I tried to explain, my voice hoarse.

She huffed with impatience, "Scar, you need to forget all of that. None of it is your fault. The only thing you could do to hurt me is to leave," she said fiercely.

"I don't know what else to do," I said quietly. "And now Cole's involved. And...I love him, Kat," I choked out. "If something happens to him because of me I couldn't live with that. I know you can't understand right now, but this is the only way I can see Jake backing off," I pleaded.

"Scarlet Malone, that is bullshit! He's going to come at them regardless. This is about more than just you – you have to understand that. You leave, and it will make everything worse!" she argued.

Well, at least I put some color back in her cheeks.

"Don't you dare walk out that door, Scar," she warned as I shot her a small smile and backed my way toward the door.

"Love you, Kat," I told her.

She gave me a wry smile. "I'm not saying goodbye to you, dumbass, I'm sending Cole after you. You're not getting rid of us that easily," she hollered as I shut the door behind me. "I'll bet my ass you're back by dinner!" I heard her shout.

I had to smile at her, throwing me attitude even as I was leaving. I wiped my face and strode out of the hospital with the clothes on my back, the medicine the doctor had prescribed and the cash in my wallet.

By nightfall, the bus dropped me off within the outskirts of Idaho. It had been an incredibly long and unpleasant day sitting on a cramped bus in unbearable pain, trying to deflect sleazebag after sleazebag.

I had enough money to stay in a motel off the freeway and I used a few bucks to get my dinner from the vending machine. I didn't want to risk going back to my place to get anything, including my car. My phone had rung about one hundred times before I finally turned it off.

I felt incredibly ill when I lay down on the scratchy comforter. I couldn't bring myself to eat. My whole body hurt and I felt utterly lost and heartbroken without Cole. I allowed myself to dissolve into tears after having held it together all day. I didn't have the energy to get up and change my bandages, though I knew I should. I simply curled up in a ball and fell asleep.

I woke up when I sensed someone else in the room.

"If you weren't hurt, I'd take you over my knee and smack your ass," Cole's deep voice growled as I jolted awake and then winced as my side rebelled against the sudden movement. "For Christ's sake, do you have any self-preservation?" he demanded with a huff.

"What are you doing here?" I asked, my voice hoarse with sleep.

"What am I doing here?" he demanded. "You cannot be believed. Jesus Christ," he bit out. "Stand up."

"Huh?" I asked.

"Stand up," he ordered, reaching for my hand.

I knew this mood and knew it best not to argue. I stood up, unable to hide my wince as he came to carefully begin unbuttoning the front of my dress. He smelled so good I had to resist the urge not to lean into him and breathe him in deep.

Despite making the choice to leave, I'd never been more relieved to see him. I'd had to at least try. Leaving was the only thing I could think to do, but it was also the last thing that I wanted. By showing up here, Cole was effectively taking that choice from me and if I was being honest in this particular instance, I would willingly hand him that.

"You didn't change these bandages. Baby, what the fuck were you thinking?" he said, more to himself than to me.

"I was exhausted," I defended myself quietly while meeting his heated gaze.

He looked up at me from his kneeling position on the floor as he reached the last button. I knew exactly what that look said, that I wouldn't be exhausted if I had stayed put.

He gently undressed me and led me to the bathroom, turning on the water for a bath. He removed my bandages as though I were made of glass, his face a mask against the emotion I saw churning in his eyes. He hadn't seen my bare skin until now, and I knew he was fighting hard not to lose it as the extent of my ordeal revealed itself.

"Get in," he continued to order as he held out a hand and helped me into the water.

I groaned in appreciation when I slipped into the warm water. It felt amazing against my tired and sore body.

"How did you find me?" I asked quietly.

"Wasn't hard, which means it wouldn't have been hard for anyone else," he replied tersely. He was seriously pissed at me.

"You're seriously pissed." I spoke my thoughts out loud.

"Doesn't even cover it," he replied without hesitation.

I nodded, accepting that fact. I deserved it and I was too exhausted to put up much of a fight anyway.

"We'll talk, and trust me, you are going to fucking hear me, but I'm too pissed right now," he said not meeting my gaze as he blotted at my skin with a soapy washcloth.

I simply nodded again, wincing slightly at his ministrations.

He watched my face carefully every time he touched me. I knew my face looked horrible and my body worse. I was surprised I didn't feel more self-conscious under his gaze, but there was no judgment in his eyes, only concern.

When he was satisfied that I was clean, he carefully dried me off and put clean bandages on. We didn't speak, and despite his obvious anger at me, I appreciated every hair on his head.

"Bed," he directed.

I turned and looked up at him, bracing myself against the emotion on his face. "I…." I didn't know how to tell him everything I felt for him. I didn't know how to explain why I left. His beautiful face, darkened with emotion regarded me for a few silent moments.

Something in my face must have conveyed some part of what I felt because his expression softened some. "Bed, baby," he said, softer this time.

I nodded.

I climbed in, careful to avoid my left side and watched him as he undressed and climbed in beside me. He didn't reach out for me, but instead he lay on his back with his arm thrown behind his head. He studied the ceiling and I tried to find sleep.

When I was just about to drift off, I had the sensation of falling. It had happened to me at the hospital as well. I cried out and jerked fully awake.

"Babe?" his deep voice asked through sleep beside me.

His quiet voice through the darkness was enough to send the tears spilling over as my body shook with the effort to keep them back. "I'm so sorry," I choked out. "I just… I don't want anything to happen to you," I said hoarsely as I heard him sigh in resignation and pull me carefully to his body. "I've lost everything, Cole. I can do it again. What I can't do is stand by and know I'm the cause for any harm that comes to you or to your family," I whispered.

"Baby," he said tenderly, his large hand stroking my back trying to soothe me while turning on the light with the other.

"We've known each other for like a minute," I exclaimed. "And already look what kind of shit I've brought down on you and on Kat," I demanded.

"Best minute of my life," he said quietly.

"What?" I asked, confused.

"Keep up, babe," he said as he chuckled. Clearly his mood had lightened. "I'm saying it doesn't matter how long we've known each other – doesn't even factor. But however long it's been, it has been the best of my life so far," he told me, kissing my head. "But this was a fucking hair-brained idea, and if you pull this shit again, I'll chain you to the bed and I won't make it fun," he threatened.

I huffed and pulled away slightly to glare at him.

He sighed and pulled me back to him, not allowing space between us. "I get the sense that I can't talk you out of feeling responsible. Not yet anyway. What I can try to get through your thick skull is that even if all this was your fault I'd still be right here, right now. You don't get this, but it doesn't matter. What matters is that any shit that may come up from your past pales in comparison to the gift of getting to be with you, baby," he said softly. "I'd take it all a thousand times over and not bat an eye. Now clearly, it's a different type of relationship, but I've known you a month and you've been making Kat's life better for over eight years, so I'd imagine she feels the exact same way I do."

I sucked in my breath at his beautiful and surprisingly tender words.

"Another thing to understand," he said, his tone taking a harder edge, "you leave, I find you. You don't get to run away Scarlet, not from me."

We regarded each other in silence for a few beats. "Thick skull?" I asked with a raised brow.

"Out of everything I just said, that's what she picks up on," he muttered to himself.

"I heard what you said," I said quietly, meeting his brilliant blue eyes.

"Then that would mean you'll promise me that you're not going to pull this shit again. Not even when shit gets real with that motherfucker," he bit out. "You don't protect me, I protect you and I can't do that properly if I'm chasing your ass across state lines," he muttered.

"Gets real?" I asked with a gulp.

"You're on a need-to-know basis with that," he answered. "But you and I both know that this shit will not fucking stand."

I nodded, resisting the urge to plead with him not to get hurt in the process. I knew he wouldn't like that.

"Promise me," he insisted.

I thought about it for a moment, taking in everything he'd said. "I promise," I replied firmly.

"Well, thank Christ for that favor," he replied sarcastically, and I jabbed him in the ribs.

We were quiet for a few moments as I lay my head

against his chest. "Kat was right," I muttered begrudgingly.

"About what?"

"Said you'd find me by dinner," I sighed in resignation.

He threw back his head and laughed out loud. "I like her, I really do."

Then he turned serious. "Baby, what was the plan here anyway? You only have the clothes on your back."

I lifted my head and met his gaze. "I have more than I had the last time," I answered quietly. "And I made out okay then."

His expression softened dramatically at my admission. "You did what almost nobody could. You made a life from nothing. But I'm in that life now and I'm not letting you slip through my fingers," he said quietly.

"I don't want you to," I admitted.

He reached out for me and pulled me back down to his chest. "Sleep, babe."

"Okay," I murmured. "I didn't want to leave, you know," I whispered.

He gave me a squeeze. "I know."

Chapter Ten

Cole had us checked out and on the road before 9 AM the next day. I'd never ridden in his truck before. I noticed somewhat absently that it was nice and well cared for. He was anxious to get back to "see to some shit" as he put it. I didn't ask what that meant. His attitude toward me was the same as always and I assumed this meant that I was forgiven. Kat and I had talked briefly. She merely laughed when I'd told her somewhat meekly that I was on the way home. Clearly she hadn't doubted Cole's tracking abilities for a moment, or his ability to haul my ass back home.

"Can I ask you something?" he asked after we'd been on the road about an hour, coffees in hand. I had just scarfed down a giant muffin. I was starved from missing dinner the night before.

From his tone I felt immediately on guard. "Okay," I answered somewhat warily.

"When we were headed to the hospital, you seemed to know a lot about making up shit to tell the nurses. I was curious why that was," he asked, his tone carefully neutral.

I sighed and looked out the window. The last thing Cole needed was more information to get him riled. Though I supposed he couldn't really be any more pissed off.

"Babe," he commanded when I took too long to answer.

"I'd rather just put that all behind me, Cole," I answered him softly.

He glanced at me briefly before he reached over and flapped my visor down so I could see myself in its mirror. "That look like the past to you sweetheart?" he asked, his tone laced with restrained anger.

I sighed, resigned. "Victor and Jake didn't like my attitude very much after my dad died," I began, looking out the window as the desert landscape shot past. "They needed me to get on board with their plan to take leadership, it would be smoother if I was behind them. The club wasn't warming to the idea the way they'd hoped. But obviously I wasn't on board, and I sure as hell wasn't going to be bullied into it either," I explained.

"So?" he prompted me to continue when I paused.

"So, they knocked me around a couple of times," I said as I shrugged and sensed him stiffen in his seat. I ignored it and forged ahead. "Tried to scare me. Knocked around a few of the other girls, too, but I took the brunt of it. I had a double target on my head since I wouldn't support them and I didn't want to be with Jake anymore. A bruised ego for a man like that is a dangerous thing."

"Knocked you around how?" Cole asked his voice deceptively soft.

I turned to look at him, his jaw was set in a firm line, but I couldn't see his eyes since he was wearing sunglasses. "Why do you want to know about this?" I asked quietly. "You can't change it. It's done. And you've already got enough anger in you about this to last a couple of decades," I tried to reason.

"Knocked you around how, Scarlet?" he repeated.

Nope, there would be no reasoning with him.

"Mostly it was just a lot of manhandling, pulling my hair, threatening me, shoving me around. But there were a few times when Jake or Victor were drunk and I got a split lip, broken finger, or bruised ribs out of those different instances. The last time... the worst time... was right before I split," I told him.

"What happened the worst time?" he demanded.

"I don't want to talk about this, Cole," I whispered firmly, my voice growing hoarse.

He surprised me by directing the truck off the highway and turning the engine off. After a few minutes of silence, he tilted his body to look at me. I looked at him with wide eyes, tears threatening to fall. It had taken me five years to finally tell Kat this story. Now Cole was demanding it after only weeks. It was a difficult prospect to consider.

He reached out his hand, cupping the back of my neck and took his sunglasses off. "Nothing you tell me would change the way I feel about you. You know that right?" he asked quietly.

Did I know that? I thought about that for a moment. We'd known each other such a short time and already so many of my past skeletons had risen up to haunt us. Cole had met each and every one with such fierce determination and not a hint of judgment. There was still part of me that believed that he was too good to be true. Perhaps it was time to finally dispel that notion.

I nodded.

"I need you to let me in, baby. And I know some of that will take more time. But I need to know what happened. You can't keep that shit bottled up."

I took in a shaky breath. I felt so raw and vulnerable with him staring so intently at me – waiting for me to divulge what only Kat knew. But I trusted him with those emotions, trusted him with everything.

I took in a shaky breath and forged ahead. "When knocking me around wasn't proving to be successful, they tried to force me...." I choked out, hating to relive the hideous ordeal. I saw Cole's jaw clench in response as he tried to keep himself under control.

Talking about it made me feel the oppressiveness of the room at the club they'd dragged me into all over again. It had smelled like stale beer and I would never forget that Black Sabbath's "Paranoid" was playing on the stereo. I'd never be able to hear that band again without reliving that horrible day.

Cole's grip on my shoulder got nearly painful before he forced his hand back to his lap for fear he'd hurt me by accident.

I took a deep fortifying breath and closed my eyes. For some reason that was the only way I could continue. "They kept laughing...." I whispered hoarsely. "Like my screaming and fighting was hilarious. But they were both high and drunk. That's probably what made it possible for me to escape with only some ripped clothes and bruises," I finished, opening my eyes but staring straight ahead. I wasn't able to look at him just yet.

"You must have put up a damn good fight," he replied quietly.

I nodded and looked down in my lap.

"Be back," he said tersely and exited the truck with alarming speed. I took in a shaky breath in the overwhelming silence of the cab and allowed him his time to cool off. I could hear my breath whipping in and out through my mouth before it began to slow, and I felt my accelerated heart rate return to a more normal speed.

It didn't take as long as I would have guessed before he was opening my door, his handsome face staring down into mine. He looked at me with such raw emotion that it nearly took my breath away as his calloused fingers stroked my face. My cheek was black and blue with some swelling, but I could tell at that moment he wasn't seeing that. He was just seeing me. Having told him my ugliest truth, and having him look at me with what could only be described as adoration, I'd never felt more free.

"Thank you for telling me," his deep voice finally said, and I knew what effort it cost him to hold it together.

"Do I have enough baggage for you yet?" I asked shakily as I laughed, wanting desperately to lighten the heavy atmosphere. Clearly Cole was in no mood for light.

He regarded me seriously and put his forehead to mine. "You have battle scars. There's a difference," he said quietly.

I wanted so badly to tell him that I loved him, but I didn't want the moment tainted by what I'd just told him. So I held it in and kissed his beautiful mouth instead, then I reached my arms around his neck, pulling him close.

"Thank you," I whispered quietly in his ear.

He simply squeezed me back as a reply. We stayed that way for many long moments before he pulled away to restart our journey home.

"Where are we going?" I asked in confusion when he didn't take my exit once we'd arrived back in town.

"My place," he answered as though it were obvious.

"But I need to go home," I protested. "I need to do

laundry and I don't have anything with me."

"You're not going home until this shit is sorted," he replied tersely.

"What?" I demanded.

"You're at my place until further notice," he added.

"Cole," I said, my tone bordering on hysteria. "I get that our relationship is far from ordinary, intensity-wise especially."

He chuckled.

"But I don't think it's a good idea for me to essentially move in after a few weeks of dating," I argued.

"Is that what this is? Dating?" he asked, the humor gone from his tone.

"What else would you call it?" I asked defensively.

"You're just gonna have to suck it up darlin'," he said without answering my question. "Your options are the clubhouse or my house. Which will it be?" he asked.

I blew out a sigh. "Your place I guess," I muttered.

"I'll try not to make it too painful for you," he said dryly, and I realized with a shock that I might have hurt his feelings.

"It's not that I don't want to be with you, honey," I said quietly. "I'm just used to being alone – I've done nothing but build walls up for eight years. It feels really foreign to have them all coming down around me," I explained.

That seemed to make him feel better.

"Get used to it," he replied with a wry smile.

Right. That was easier said than done.

"I'll have one of the boys bring your things later on," he said as we pulled up to the curb.

"You're going to let one of your boys pick out my underwear?" I asked with a raised brow.

"Scratch that. I'll bring your things later on," he amended, throwing an arm around me as we walked into the house.

I laughed out loud and squeezed his waist.

"Okay, ground rules," he said seriously once he'd closed his front door and I'd put my purse down on the island.

I raised my brows at this change of topic.

"The house is on radar. One of the boys will be keeping an eye out any time I'm not here," he explained. "You don't go anywhere by yourself. You wait for someone to take you.

"No," he said and shook his head when I opened my mouth to protest. "This shit is non-negotiable." He waited for me to clamp my mouth shut before continuing. "Next, work. I'd much prefer you didn't work, but I know what a pain in my ass you'll be if I force that so someone will take you and pick you up. Same goes for the gym."

I rolled my eyes thoroughly annoyed at the prospect of having babysitters.

"I need you to take this shit seriously, baby," he said sternly, holding my face in both hands and stooping slightly to meet my eyes. "This is no fucking joke, and I will be damned if there is any opportunity for those motherfuckers to ever lay a hand on you again. Do you understand?"

"Yes," I said softly, immediately conceding. "Can Kat come keep me company when I'm on house arrest?" I quipped.

He smiled and nodded.

Well, at least there was that.

"Do you feel okay? Maybe you should lie down," he said worriedly.

"I'm fine," I assured him.

"I have to head out for a few hours, but I'll be back as soon as I can."

"Yes, dear." I smiled sweetly.

"Pain in my ass," he muttered, smiling. He captured my mouth then in an unexpected passionate kiss. "Be good," he whispered against my mouth, making my knees weak.

"Okay," I whispered back, breathlessly. I would have agreed to just about anything at that moment.

Once he took off, I flopped down on the couch and called Kat. "I feel like a child on a timeout," I complained.

She laughed. "I'll come entertain you soon. I'm just down the street at Sal's."

"Oh?" I asked suggestively.

"It would seem these biker boys are a bit overprotective," she muttered.

I burst out laughing. She had no idea.

"You feeling okay?" I asked, my tone serious.

"Yeah. I'm fine," she assured me. "Just some wicked road rash, same as you. I got off easier. I'm not sporting a black eye," she muttered.

"Thank God," I sighed.

"Let me just wrap up a couple of things here and I'll be over," she told me.

"Wrap up a couple of things?" I replied cheekily, trying hard to suppress my laughter and failing miserably.

"Bite me," she said as she giggled. "See you in a few."

After we hung up, I wandered around Cole's place unsure what to do with myself. His house was comfortable, but it certainly didn't feel like home. I grew tired of pacing and flopped on the couch to watch some TV until Kat showed up.

I heard the roar of a bike not too much later and I smiled to myself. I got up to let her in and waved to Sal who gave me a chin lift as he sat idling at the curb.

"Remember what I told you," he barked to Kat over the engine noise.

"Yeah, yeah," she hollered back, waving her hand at him as we shut the door.

I raised my brow at her as I locked the door and reset the alarm.

She rolled her eyes. "Same shit I'm sure Cole told you. No going anywhere, be careful... blah, blah," she grumbled.

I laughed at her attitude and without asking I started making us each a cocktail. "What's going on with you two anyway?" I asked curiously as she sat at the bar.

She sighed. "I'm done for," she admitted. "I've never felt like this about a guy, but part of me is terrified that he's only being so protective because of the whole alpha male thing. "Girl, mine. You no touch," she grunted, imitating a caveman.

I laughed a loud belly laugh. It felt great.

"Part of me is worried that once all this blows over, he'll lose interest," she admitted, her tone serious. "He's been taking great care of me," she added quietly.

I smiled warmly, pleased to hear that. "He was chasing after you before this happened. You were at the club when this bullshit started. That's huge," I reminded her.

"I guess," she muttered.

"It is," I said firmly, taking a much needed sip of my drink.

"So did Cole tan your hide or what?" she wanted to

know, and I knew she wanted to change the subject.

"At first he wanted to," I admitted. "But then I explained why I did it and I think he understood. I'm pretty sure I'm forgiven," I said as I shrugged. "I told him about how things were with Jake and Victor," I practically whispered.

Her eyes grew wide. "Even...?"

"Yep."

"Holy shit, did he completely lose his mind?"

"Actually, no. I was kind of shocked. He held it together really well," I told her as we moved over to the couch and faced each other, both trying to get comfortable on the soft leather.

"I'm impressed," she murmured. "How did it feel to tell him?"

I grimaced. "Obviously it sucked to relive that shit. But I guess in the end it was somewhat freeing to tell someone other than you, and to have him be so great about it."

"He loves you, you know," she said softly.

I bit my lip. "I would like to think that's true."

"I know it's true," she said firmly. "When you left, I thought he was going to literally murder anyone who held him up even a second in taking off to go get your stupid ass," she told me and laughed when I swatted at her. "He was so worried."

"Well, he got me back quickly enough, and it would seem as though I'm to be a house guest indefinitely." I wrinkled my nose.

"I'm not surprised. I promise to come visit you all the time," she said and clinked her glass with mine.

"Sal isn't chaining you to the bed?" I asked with a raised brow.

She shook her head. "I talked him out of it. I'm not a

target like you are. It was just wrong place, wrong time."

"Yeah, but Kat, you're my roommate. Someone might think I'm still there," I interjected worriedly.

She waved me off. "I may not be under house arrest, but that doesn't mean Sal isn't keeping a close eye. I'll be fine."

I let the topic go for the moment but I was hardly pacified.

We drank martinis and gabbed until Sal came by to pick Kat up. I resisted asking him if he'd seen Cole, not wanting to seem like a clichéd housewife. But when he wasn't home by 10 PM that night, I called him. It went straight to voicemail. My brow wrinkled wondering where he was. He hadn't made it seem like he'd be gone that long. I still didn't have anything with me, so I borrowed one of his T-shirts and a toothbrush, and then crawled into a very empty feeling bed.

When I rolled over at 2 AM and found that his side of the bed was still cold, I got really worried. I called his cell again and when I still got no answer, I called Kat. Obviously I woke her up, but she put Sal on the phone after I explained about Cole.

"He's working through some shit. He's fine," Sal told me, making my blood run cold.

"Working through some shit?" I asked, my tone arctic. What the hell did that mean?

"He's safe, he's at the club," he told me, his tone softer.

"Okay, well that's where I'm going then," I huffed, hauling myself out of bed.

"You aren't," Sal argued.

"I am," I retorted. "Hank's out front. I'm sure he'll take me," I added. The poor guy was probably bored to tears anyway.

"Fuck," he clipped. "I'll be there in ten minutes." I didn't take it as a great sign that Sal was insisting on taking me if I was going, but I pushed that worry to the back of my mind and got dressed.

"This is a bad idea," he informed me once he dragged his ass out of bed to come get me in his pickup truck.

"Oh well," I said as I shrugged, feigning indifference as I looked out the window. The truth was that I was scared out of my ever loving mind at what I would find at the club. But I had to know what kind of shit he was working through. If he couldn't work things through with me then we had a serious problem. And God help me, and him, if he was working through anything with someone else.

I spotted him immediately when we walked in. His back was to us, body hunched over the bar as he sipped what looked like whiskey. I was pacified to see he was alone. And even more so when I saw him immediately brush off a woman who walked over to him and tried to put a hand flirtatiously on his shoulder. Clearly this wasn't about anything other than being in his own head, deeply in his own head. There were a few other guys shooting pool but it was really late, or early, and the place was pretty quiet.

"Penny for your thoughts?" I asked quietly, pulling up the stool beside him.

His eyebrows rose in surprise. "What are you doing here?" his eyes were bloodshot but his speech wasn't slurred.

"Couldn't sleep without you," I said, pulling the bottle over and taking a swig. He turned back and stared into his drink. "Find what you're looking for in there?" I asked softly.

I'd never seen him like this. He wasn't angry or his typical alpha self. He was contemplative and almost… sad.

"You shouldn't be here," he said quietly and his words sent a stab of pain through my heart.

"Why?" I spoke past the lump in my throat.

He didn't answer. He sat quietly and swirled the liquid in his glass.

"You're always asking me to let you in," I said quietly. "You need to do the same for me. I want to be here for you," I added, putting my hand over his.

"I can't do this right now," he said, his tone turning firm and almost cold.

I pulled my hand back. "Do what?" I demanded, hurt searing through me like a flame. "Do what, Cole?" I demanded again when he didn't answer me.

"I can't fucking look at you right now, alright?" he clipped loudly.

I was so shocked by what he said that it took a moment for it to register. But as the words rushed over me, my face flamed in humiliation and hurt. A few of the guys had turned to look in surprise at our exchange and my cheeks flamed brighter still.

I opened myself up to him that morning, allowed him to see parts of me I'd buried deep and held protected. And this is how he repaid me, by making me feel complete and utter shame.

I kept staring at him in complete shock and pain for a few seconds before I stood up on shaking legs and put my purse on my shoulder. He didn't spare me a glance as I walked away. My throat was close to bursting with the size of the lump lodged there. I walked woodenly past Sal, who stood with his arms crossed, eyes narrowed on Cole.

"I'm not going back there!" I cried when Sal had caught up with me.

"Okay, get in the truck," he said quietly.

"Promise me you won't make me go back to Cole's house. I want to go home," I whimpered.

"I can't do that, honey. You know your place isn't safe. You can stay in my guest room. Kat's already at my place," he reminded me.

I simply nodded, trying desperately to hold back the onslaught of hysteria. I didn't want to break down in front of Sal. I'd suffered enough humiliation already. The drive felt unbearably long, but we finally pulled up in front of his place. He ushered me inside and led me to his guest bedroom.

"I'm sorry, Scarlet. That was fucked up," he muttered. I could tell he was out of his depth. We didn't even know each other that well. But I knew him well enough to know that dealing with emotion wasn't his strong suit. "Get you anything?" he asked, his tone concerned and hesitant.

"No, thanks," I managed, barely holding it together.

He simply nodded and closed the door quietly behind him. The moment I heard the door click, my eyes filled with tears and I stifled a sob. I lay down on the bed and tried to be quiet as my body shook with the force of my tears. It was mere moments before I heard the door quietly open and felt Kat's body slide into bed with me. She put her arms around me as I faced the wall and sobbed into the pillow.

"What happened?" she asked quietly after I'd been sobbing for an indeterminate amount of time.

"I... God, I have no idea!" I cried, my breath coming out in gasps. "He didn't come home, so I got worried and I called here to see if Sal had seen him. He said Cole was at the club so I went to go talk to him. And he was just so... cold!" I sobbed. "He said he couldn't look at me, that I shouldn't be there. It was like he was a completely different person!" I wailed, no longer able to control the volume of my distress.

I heard Kat's intake of breath as she squeezed me tighter.

"After everything I told him today, how could he hurt me like that? I have never felt so humiliated or ashamed. He can't look at me?" I cried. "How could he ever say something like that to me?"

"Oh, honey, I'm so sorry," she soothed.

I started crying again and couldn't speak. She just held me and whispered soothing words that I didn't understand through my haze.

"It's over," I mumbled, my breath hiccupping. "I don't ever want to see him again," I said vehemently.

Kat didn't say anything but just kept rubbing my back.

"What I don't get is why he went to all the effort of dragging me back here when just hours later he was so capable of such cold indifference?" I asked.

"I don't know, sweetie," she said softly.

"I can't believe it's over," I mumbled hoarsely.

She continued to rub my back, murmuring soothing words.

I must have finally drifted off because the next thing I knew I heard yelling from the living room.

"You have completely gutted her!" I heard Kat shrieking. "There is no way in hell I'm letting you back there. She finally lets someone in and this how you fucking repay her?"

"Get out of my way," Cole's deep voice boomed.

"Put a hand on my woman and we've got problems, man," I heard Sal interject. "You need to go home and cool off."

"Why the fuck is she under your roof?" Cole demanded angrily. How on earth had he thought he'd go home to find me there? I wondered how drunk he must be.

"Because after how you treated her, there was no way she was willingly going back to your place, and I wasn't going to let her go back to hers. So here she is," Sal stated. "You need to get your fucking head together man. I don't know what that was about tonight but if you care about her, and I know you do, you'll go home."

"She doesn't want to see you, Cole," Kat added angrily. "You'll be lucky if she wants to see you again at all."

"Fuck," I heard Cole clip. "Fuck!" he bellowed again a moment later, his emotion apparent even through the walls.

"Go sleep it off man," Sal instructed.

"It doesn't feel right, leaving without her," I heard him say flatly.

"Well you're going to have to, asshole," I heard Kat hiss.

"Babe, bedroom," Sal ordered.

She must have done as she was told because I didn't hear a reply.

Sal's voice dropped a few notches and I couldn't hear what he was saying anymore. But whatever he said must have pacified Cole to some extent because I heard the front door open and shut, then all was quiet.

I listened to the sound of my ragged breathing, my heart pounding in my chest as it had been throughout the whole exchange. I hadn't expected him to come here for me. I felt so confused, I couldn't process anything aside from the fact that I was deeply hurt.

I managed to get some sleep, though very little. Mostly I just lay on my back and stared up at the ceiling, my eyes burning from tears and exhaustion. Kat slipped in again in the morning and I looked over at her without emotion.

"Did you sleep?" she whispered, crawling back in bed with me.

"Barely," I murmured hoarsely.

"Did you hear?" she asked, referring to the night before.

I nodded. "Most of it. I don't get how in the hell he thought I would be in his bed when he got home. He must be out of his mind," I said.

She shook her head. "I don't know what was going through his mind either, other than him being so completely wrecked that we wouldn't let him back here to see you."

"Thank God you didn't," I breathed. We were quiet for a few beats before I took a deep breath. "I don't know what to do now," I whispered, my eyes welling back up.

"What do you mean?" she asked softly.

"All I want is to just go home. But I know he won't allow that, none of them will. But if I thought I wanted to disappear before, that was nothing compared to now."

"I'm sure Sal will let you stay here," she suggested.

I shook my head. "I don't want him in the middle of this. It wouldn't be fair. He and Cole go way back."

"Connie?" she suggested.

I bit my lip. "Yeah, maybe that would work for a little bit." I sighed.

"I'll call her," she said immediately. I knew she was

desperate to do something to help. She got up to call Connie and I continued my scrutiny of the ceiling.

I hadn't moved by the time Kat returned. "Connie said you can stay with her. I filled her in a little, I hope you don't mind," she added.

I simply nodded, feeling completely devoid of emotion. I felt utterly numb.

"Come on, Scar, let's get you up and into the shower. Then we'll get some of your stuff and take you to Connie's," she told me, pulling me up and practically shoving me into the bathroom.

I felt like a robot as I went through the motions of getting dressed. Kat let me borrow some clothes. I stared at the breakfast she put in front of me, unable to take a bite. I saw Sal and Kat exchange glances, but I didn't have it in me to put on a show. I was wrecked, no sense in hiding it.

Finally, after what felt like an eternity, I was all set up in Connie's guest room. We'd stopped briefly at the apartment and Kat had run in to get some of my stuff. I sat on the bed and stared into space. Kat had offered to stay with me but I waved her off. I needed time alone and she had a life to live. Connie hadn't asked questions, but had simply hugged me and showed me to my room. I was utterly grateful that she didn't hover. Finally, I curled up in a ball on top of the bedspread fully clothed and fell asleep.

Chapter Eleven

When I woke up it was pitch black out and the clock told me it was just after midnight. My stomach growled. I hadn't eaten in over 24 hours, but I ignored it. I clicked on the light and forced myself to sit up. I sat there a while trying to get my head sorted when a soft knock sounded at the door.

"Hey," Connie said quietly, peeking her head in. "I saw your light on, how are you?"

I gave her a weak smile. "Been better."

"You should eat something," she said softly.

"Later," I shook my head. What I really needed were my painkillers, but if I took them on an empty stomach I knew I'd get sick.

"Listen, I know it isn't my place, but whatever happened – Cole looks about as good as you do," she said quietly. "He's already come by several times to try to see you. I told him to give it another day," she said quietly.

"Cole can go to hell," I shot out, surprised by my anger, but relieved to feel it. I was tired of being so desperately sad.

She looked at me carefully before nodding simply.

"I think I'll just watch some TV for a little bit if that's

okay," I said while standing up to stretch my stiff limbs.

"Whatever you need, babe," she said. "I just got home from work and was planning to head to Wes's. Will you be okay by yourself?" she asked worriedly.

"Totally," I said as I nodded. In fact, it sounded great to have the place to myself. "I really appreciate you putting me up."

"Don't mention it. I'm barely ever here. You're welcome to stay as long as you want," she said with a warm smile.

I got changed into my pajamas and grabbed a cozy throw blanket. I curled up on the couch and flipped on the TV as Connie gathered her stuff and headed out.

My phone chirped with the tenth text of the day from Cole, and I reached over and turned the thing off without even looking at what his message said. He couldn't act that way with me and then just bombard me until I gave in. I needed space and time to collect myself. I'd been through a hell of a lot the last few days and I needed to feel safe and secure. At the moment, that meant being alone.

I spent the next day pretty much... well, wallowing. The two times I tried to leave the apartment to get some air, I was soon followed by some badass biker. I was in no mood to have a chaperone, so each time I just turned back around and huffed my way back into the house. What I really wanted was to be able to run off the confusion and hurt that I was feeling but my injuries prevented that option. Cole was giving me my space. He'd only texted once that day and because I missed him, I couldn't help but look at it. It was simple and to the point.

"Miss you babe."

I missed him, too. It hadn't even been two full days, but I did. He'd become the center of my universe in such a short time. My heart belonged to him and I knew that it always would. But he'd hurt me during a time when I was most fragile and I was far from ready to answer any of his calls.

Kat stopped by to inform me that Cole felt like utter shit. He told her so himself when he asked her how I was. She was still pissed at him, but even she had given into his persuasive tendencies and seemed to be gently suggesting that I talk to him. I'd given her an outright "no," which had stopped her from pressing me.

Dinnertime came and went, but I wasn't hungry. I'd been mindlessly watching TV for a while when I heard the low rumble of a motorcycle that started in the distance but kept coming closer. My heart started thudding in my throat at the unmistakable sound of it stopping out front. A knock sounded at the door moments later.

"Shit," I whispered to myself. I sunk deeper into the couch, hoping that he'd just go away.

"Not going away till you open the door, babe," I heard his deep voice boom through the door.

"Shit," I clipped, hauling off the couch and stalking to the front door. I took a deep breath, trying to calm my raging emotions and opened the door.

I hated that he was easily the most handsome man I'd ever seen. I hated that even though I was beyond pissed at him, my body still responded to him. I couldn't help myself from taking him in, my eyes roaming over his face. He did look tired, his eyes were red and he clearly hadn't shaved in a while. Not that he did that regularly anyway. I noticed him doing the same thing, taking in my swollen, red eyes, my hair thrown up in a sloppy bun. If he didn't want to look at me before there certainly wasn't anything good to look at now.

"Gonna let me in?" he asked quietly.

"Fuck no," I replied without hesitation.

He sighed and looked off to the side, biting his lip as though he was choosing his words carefully.

"What I said, it came out wrong," he started.

"How the hell does 'I can't look at you' come out wrong?" I demanded, thankful that my anger hadn't yet deserted me for despair.

"My thoughts were all fucked up. I was drinking and having a really fucking hard time with everything that happened to you." He blew out a breath. "In that moment, looking at you just reminded me how I didn't protect you – knowing what he did to you and that he was able to get at you again," he admitted. "Looking at you reminded me that I failed you," he said, his voice raw. "It had nothing to do with you and everything to do with me," he said quietly.

"Okay," I nodded.

"Okay?" he asked incredulously.

"Yeah, I understand. My shit is heavy and it's more than most people could handle. I just thought maybe you could," I said with feigning indifference. "But, I get it. No hard feelings."

His eyes narrowed. "What do you mean, no hard feelings?" he demanded.

"I mean, no hard feelings. Take care of yourself," I said, starting to close the door.

"What the fuck?" he demanded, putting a hand forcefully on the front door preventing me from closing it.

"We're done, Cole," I said as though it was obvious.

"Come again?" his voice was deceptively soft as he stared down at me.

"We're done," I said again, determined to sound far more confident than I actually felt.

"The fuck we are," he growled.

"Oh no," I said, my anger flaring. "This is not the time for you to assert your macho bullshit. You do not get to decide this. You already made your decision when you disappeared into a whiskey bottle and told me some really fucking hurtful shit following one of the worst weeks I've had in my life!" I exclaimed, my voice rising. "Now it's my turn and I say we are done," I said emphatically.

I glared at him and he stared back at me. I watched his entire face change from frustration to something close to reverence. I braced for what he was about to say.

"We aren't. We'll never be done," he returned without hesitation. "I'm yours and you're mine. I said something I didn't mean, it came out entirely wrong. And I'm sorry I hurt you… really fucking sorry, baby. But we'll work it out. There just isn't another option," he said.

I narrowed my eyes at him. "Let me clue you in. The other option is for us to be done!" I shrieked, trying to close the door on him again, but he quickly put his boot in the way.

"We can't be done. I'm in love with you," he said quietly.

Dammit. Those words caused my anger to desert me, and tears immediately filled my eyes. "How can you say that to me?" I whispered hoarsely. "You basically force me to tell you some really unpleasant shit and then hours later, you can't look at me? That's not love, Cole," I said as I shook my head.

His eyes softened as he looked at my now tear-streaked face.

"No one has ever loved anyone as much as I love you," he said, undeterred by my comment. "I admit, I let that shit fester. The fact that fucker ever laid a hand on you is eating me up inside. The fact that he grabbed you right from under my fucking nose combined with everything you told me yesterday is really fucking hard for me to swallow, I admit. But I should have just let it out. I was trying to protect you by holding it in, that was a mistake. It won't happen again."

I simply stared at him, not allowing my reaction to his words show.

He blew out a breath. "Baby, there's no one else in this world I'd rather look at than you. You are the most beautiful thing in my world, whether you're all done up to hit the town or as you are now, tearful and exhausted. In that moment, I just couldn't see past my own shit," he said and paused for a minute, assessing me closely. "I can see that you're not ready to move past this. But I'm not leaving, whether I'm in bed with you or on the couch. We can talk more tomorrow," he said firmly.

"Fine," I grumbled, my shoulders slumping. I knew he meant what he said and I just didn't have it in me to fight him anymore. "The couch it is." I gestured to it. I felt exhausted by our exchange and just wanted to be alone. I could feel my resolve wavering and that scared me. I walked away from him, leaving the door open behind me and heard him follow me inside. I clicked the TV off, and without a look back I went into Connie's guest room and shut the door.

I curled back up into my now-familiar ball. I tried so hard to stifle the sobs that inevitably started. With everything that had happened the last few days and how little sleep I'd been getting, I was utterly unable to keep my emotion in check. When I heard the door open I squeezed my eyes shut.

"Scoot over, baby," his deep voice ordered softly.

"No," I choked.

"Not gonna lay out there and listen to you in here cryin' and not do anything about it. Scoot," he said again, bending down to gently shift me over. He crawled in behind me and pulled my body to his so that we were spooning.

I hated how amazing it felt to have his strong arms wrapped around me – hated how much I needed him, how much I loved him. I wanted to force him away from me or to remain stiff in his arms, but I simply couldn't fight it.

"Love you, baby," he whispered, his mouth at my ear. "I'm sorry." He squeezed me tighter.

I merely hiccupped as my tears subsided and I started to drift off.

When I woke, I realized that Cole was still beside me and I could tell from his breathing that he was awake. Great. I was facing away from him and I stared at the wall trying to collect myself.

"How long do you want to pretend you're sleepin'?" his deep voice rumbled.

Dammit.

"A little bit longer," I answered.

He chuckled before rolling toward me and he pulled me back toward his body. "Baby, do you honestly think what I was working out that night had anything to do with how I feel about you?" he asked, his deep, sleepy voice causing an involuntary reaction between my legs.

"No," I answered honestly. I'd had time to think about this somewhat rationally. I knew he loved me and that he was just lashing out, but that in itself was part of the problem. "But I do think that if you can't work shit out with me then we don't have much to work with," I answered quietly. "Leaving the house like everything's fine and then not even calling, just disappearing into a whiskey bottle and lashing out at me… I'm not going to put up with that shit, Cole."

"I know," he answered without hesitation.

"I still need some time," I whispered.

"Can't give you that," he answered immediately.

"Why the hell not?" I demanded.

"Waited thirty years for you. I'm done waiting," he whispered, his breath warm on my ear, making me shiver. "Baby, I'm going to act like a jackass sometimes. We're still getting to know each other. And neither one of us has had a healthy relationship to learn from before. But we're going to learn how to do this together. So no, I can't give you space. What I can give you is a promise that I will try my damnedest not to hurt you and to handle you with care. I'll protect you with everything I've got, and I'm not going to hold back who I am – not even if it might protect you in the short term. Because in the long term, it'll break us down," he said emphatically. "That's what happened the other night and I learned from it. I need to find a balance between not scaring the shit out of you, but also not burying shit so deep that it festers," he mused. "It's just not something I've ever had to consider before."

"What were you holding back?" I asked turning to face him, his blue-eyed gaze mere inches from mine.

He sighed. "I'd already had a fairly loose hold of my temper since this whole bullshit started, but when you told me about what those fuckers did to you and what they tried to do...."he trailed off as his jaw got tight. "I had to bottle that shit so tight, I've never felt anything like it," he explained.

I nodded, biting my lip and looking away.

"Hey," he said quietly, tilting my chin back toward him. "I'm glad you told me. I needed for you to tell me. I don't ever want you to keep shit like that from me," he told me vehemently.

"Even if it means you can't look at me?" I croaked out, my eyes filling with tears. God, I was so tired of crying.

"Baby, it was never you I couldn't face," he replied. "I fucked up, I'm sorry," he said, his eyes burning with sincerity.

I looked at this man who had put everything on the line for me. Who made me feel things I never knew I could – who loved me with a ferocity that I never thought I'd experience. I knew with that kind of intensity that I'd occasionally get burned. But Cole had made me realize that I'd rather be in the fire than out in the cold.

"Okay," I replied quietly.

He kissed me then, slow and sweet. My mouth opened under his and my limbs liquefied as his tongue brushed with mine. I'd missed him more than I wanted to admit.

He squeezed me tight. "Come home."

"Home?" I asked dubiously.

He rolled his eyes. "My place, babe."

"Oh, right."

"Are you not comfortable at my place?" he asked with a raised brow.

My eyes slid to the side as I debated how to answer him. There wasn't anything wrong with his place, but for the time being it represented the fact that I couldn't go home. I decided to keep this piece of information to myself, though.

"No, it's fine. I just miss my place, my things," I murmured.

"I want you to feel comfortable, bring whatever you want over. Hell, redecorate for all I care," he said with a chuckle.

"That's not necessary," I scoffed, wincing slightly as I shifted to my back.

He leaned up over me, his rough hands lightly tracing my face. "Your bruise looks much better," he murmured, gazing down at me tenderly.

"Yeah," I agreed quietly.

"How about the rest?"

I didn't miss the double meaning of his words. "Getting there," I told him honestly.

"Your strength completely slays me," he whispered. My eyes opened in shock. "You completely beguile me, my little warrior," he said as he kissed me softly.

Well, that was pretty damn amazing. "Let's get up and get you back to my place. I've been ornery as all hell not having you with me," he admitted.

Selfishly, I sort of loved that.

I took a quick shower, redressed my wounds, and put on the clothes that Kat had thrown together for me. I left Connie a note thanking her profusely for putting me up. Cole loaded his truck up with my things and I marveled at his ability to get me back so quickly, yet again. The man had my number that was for sure.

"When's the last time you ate?" he asked as he fired the truck up, looking over at me.

I bit my lip, trying to remember.

He sighed, exasperated. "The fact that you can't remember says it all. Breakfast is the first matter of business," he said, eyeing me with a possessive look. I knew his protective instincts extended to all things concerning me, including my appetite.

I smiled at my overprotective alpha. "Sounds good," I agreed readily.

And over coffee and a ginormous breakfast, I started to feel more like myself.

Cole watched as I shoveled food into my mouth. "I've never seen you eat like this," he commented, eyeing me with regret. I knew it bothered him that I was obviously so starving.

I shrugged, not wanting to make a big thing of it as his large hand engulfed mine across the table. "That's the last time you get upset enough to skip so many meals," he grunted more to himself than to me.

I squeezed his hand reassuringly. "It's done, babe. I'm fine." And I was. I knew he was dealing with a feeling of powerlessness that he was unaccustomed to and that he wouldn't take it out on me again. And, he loved me. I continued to hear him say the words over and over again in my head.

"What's on for today?" I asked, changing the subject.

"I'm hanging with you," he said simply, without hesitation.

I smiled, pleased at the thought. "That sounds good. I just have to work at six."

He scowled. "You're scheduled already? And for the late shift?" he asked incredulously. "Don't you think you should take some more time off?"

The truth was that I'd love to take more time, but my

bank account wouldn't allow for it. "Can't," I answered evasively, hoping he'd leave it at that as he settled our bill and we headed out into the sunshine.

"Why not?" he demanded lightly, opening the passenger door for me and leaning in the doorframe as I buckled myself in.

I shrugged casually, wanting desperately for him to drop it, and feeling distracted by the muscles flexing in his arms as he peered down at me. I put my hand to his chest, and pulled his T-shirt so that he was forced to lean down to me. I kissed him with nothing of the soft tenderness of the morning. He responded immediately, taking over the kiss as his body pressed into mine.

"This wouldn't be your attempt to distract me now would it?" he asked against my lips.

I simply smiled and kissed him again until our breathing was labored. "Better get you home before we get arrested for indecent exposure," he growled as he pulled away.

"This is hardly indecent," I scoffed.

"It's about to be," he answered, his fierce eyes making my toes curl.

"Oh," I breathed.

"We're not done talkin'," he warned as he closed my passenger door and came around the front of the truck.

I was afraid of that.

We drove to his place in comfortable silence as I looked out the window mulling over the past few days and what a whirlwind they had been. When we walked into his place I was momentarily stunned as I eyed the boxes of my things piled in the corner. Taking a look around the room, I noticed that my favorite throw blanket was now on his couch. My books were sitting on the media cabinet.

I noted more boxes when I entered the master bedroom.

"Um, this doesn't look like you grabbed just a few of my things," I noted, my voice sounding a bit panicky.

He came to stand behind me, placing his hands on my shoulders, "No, it's basically all of your things," he admitted, undeterred by my impending freak out. "I wanted you to be comfortable here, babe. Now all your things are here. I left the unpacking to you so that you can put your things where you want them. I just cleared some space in my dresser and the closet," he said as he shrugged, as though he were talking about something as casual as what we were going to have for dinner.

"But... we're not moving in together," I protested.

He grinned. "You just haven't agreed yet."

"But," I protested again completely at a loss.

He moved to stand in front of me stooping down slightly so that we were eye to eye. "You still have your apartment darlin', for as long as you want it. All of these things can easily be moved back there in a few hours if need be," he assured me. "Hell, if it makes you feel better don't unpack," he said nonchalantly, though I could tell the idea bothered him. "I don't want you to feel trapped, but I do want you here with me and I want that badly," he admitted.

I bit my lip, looking beyond him at the boxes. Part of me wanted that badly, too. There wasn't anywhere else I'd rather be than sleeping beside Cole every night. But it was so fast and there was so much already muddling my head. I just didn't have it in me at the moment to process it all. I couldn't even tell him I loved him, though I did with everything I had.

Instead of sharing all of this, I simply nodded, ready to

accept the compromise. He took me in his arms gently and kissed the top of my head. "What do you feel like doing?" he asked quietly.

I sighed. "Honestly, I'm exhausted. If I'm going to work tonight, I'd better rest today," I told him. Between my hospital stay and sleeping in so many unfamiliar places the last few nights, I hadn't had a decent night's sleep in close to a week.

He was quiet for a moment and I could tell he was biting his tongue about my plan to go to work. Instead he nodded. "Okay, to bed with you then," he said gently.

"Would you lay with me for just a little bit?" I asked while meeting his tender gaze.

"Sure," he agreed with a small smile.

I gingerly removed my clothes, slipped into a long nightshirt that was soft on my skin, and I crawled under the covers. It was just after noon, but I had no doubt I could sleep the day away. Cole crawled in beside me after removing his T-shirt and jeans. I immediately rolled on my good side toward his reassuring warmth. He smelled so good, and despite my exhaustion and throbbing side, I felt the familiar tingle between my legs as his hand stroked my hip. I felt his firm body beneath my fingers, and I allowed my hand to wander from his chest down to his washboard abs, then to his thigh, teasing him slightly. I heard his quick intake of breath and I smiled to myself as my cheek lay pressed against his chest. There was no mistaking the swell that immediately filled his boxer briefs. I felt wetness between my legs at the sight and I reached out to stroke him.

"I thought you were tired," his deep voice rasped.

"Not that tired."

"Fuck. Thank God," he hissed through clenched teeth as I began to stroke him. He wrapped his hand around the back of my head, pulling my lips to his. His tongue met mine and the kiss went wild, all traces of subtlety gone. It had been several days since we'd been together and the forced abstinence was clear in his kiss. He growled into my mouth as my grip got firmer around him. He pulled my hand away, moving over me, his mouth covering my nipple over my nightshirt.

I arched off the bed, sighing in pleasure as he sucked me further into his mouth. He moved down my body sliding my panties down my legs and tossing them to the floor. Then his mouth was on me, and he licked and sucked until I was crying out his name.

"Cole," I called, my voice ragged. "I need you inside me," I begged desperately.

He lifted his head and his intense gaze met mine. Something passed between us in that moment. His gaze was filled with a promise, not only of the moments to come but of something far more. I couldn't say how I knew that, I just did, and the knowledge of it nearly moved me to tears.

"Now, please," I called again.

He moved up over me, careful not to touch or rub against my bad side and slowly guided himself inside of me.

"You feel so good, baby," he groaned.

"Harder," I demanded raggedly as he glided in and out.

"I don't want to hurt you," he replied, his own voice hoarse.

"You won't," I assured him, wrapping my legs around him, pulling him into me.

Any trace of self-control he'd been holding onto was quickly abandoned as he slammed into me, eliciting a noise from my throat that I didn't even recognize. It was only moments before I felt a wave of ecstasy that rose up and crashed back down, sending such forceful shocks through my body that a single sob escaped.

"Fuck," I heard him gasp before he followed close behind me, collapsing onto my good side, his breath warm on my neck. "Okay?" he asked, his voice ragged.

"Yeah," I breathed, still trying to come back fully to my senses.

He rolled off of me and pulled me toward him, tucking me into his side. Being tucked close to Cole where I felt so safe and protected, I was able to forget my troubles momentarily and just breathe him in. How I ever thought I could do without this was beyond me. He stroked my hair as we lay not speaking and I felt myself begin to drift off.

When I woke up it was dark outside and I bolted upright in a panic. I'd completely over slept. It was nearly six o'clock – I should have been out the door already.

"Shit," I hissed, pulling on my jeans and whirling around the room, looking for my shirt.

Cole came to lean in the doorway, his arms crossed over his broad chest.

"I'm late," I exclaimed unnecessarily. "Why didn't you wake me up?" I demanded, finding my work shirt in a heap near my suitcase.

"Because you needed to sleep. I called your boss, he agreed that you need at least another night off to recuperate," he explained calmly.

"What? You called Pete?" I demanded while still topless, holding my shirt in my hand. "Why did you do that? I told you that I need to work!" I said, feeling somewhat desperate. My bills were piling up. I didn't have the luxury of an extra night to recuperate.

"And I told you to take more time," he replied, his eyes doing a body sweep. "You need to change your bandage," he added calmly.

"Fuck my bandage. I'm going to work," I huffed, trying to hide my wince as I pulled my shirt a bit too roughly over my body.

"For Christ's sake, you're going to reopen your fucking wounds. Would you please relax?" he growled.

"You relax!" I exclaimed. "I have rent to pay, a car payment! My utilities will get turned off. And I haven't even allowed myself to think about the hospital bills," I cried as I tried to whirl past him to the bathroom.

"Is that what this is about?" he asked, his tone gentle with sudden understanding, his grip firm on my arm not allowing me to pass.

I blew out a frustrated breath and met his gaze. "Of course it is. You think there's some sort of magic solution to paying bills aside from working?" I demanded and immediately narrowed my eyes when I saw his expression. "Oh no. No way." I shook my head adamantly. "I've been taking care of myself for a long time, Cole. I don't need any charity," I added coolly.

"Jesus you're a pain in the ass," he sighed while looking up at the ceiling as though for divine providence. "It's not charity, babe. I love you. You're mine to take care of and that's what I'm going to do, whether you fight me kicking and screaming the whole way or not."

"You're not paying my bills," I demanded.

"Too late." He seemed to be enjoying this.

"What do you mean too late?" I cried shrilly. "You can't just take over like that!" I ranted. "It's my decision when I work and how I pay my bills. Emphasis on I," I bit out, shaking my arm out of his grip. I couldn't say for certain why the fact that he wanted to take care of me financially panicked me to such a degree. Maybe it was that I was afraid of relying on him. Maybe it was the testament of what this type of gesture meant. Either way, I was panicking.

"Babe, relax," he said again.

"I can't relax," I gulped. "I can't get used to this."

"Used to what?" he asked gently.

"Used to someone else taking care of me. The only person who ever did was my dad and then he was just... gone," I gulped again, trying hard to swallow the lump in my throat. "It's hard enough to know I love you," I said before I could get the words back. "And now you want me to unpack and I just can't think about..."

"What did you say?" he interrupted quietly.

"About unpacking?" I asked, feigning innocence and looking away from him as he pulled me close.

He put his finger under my chin, forcing my gaze to his. "Before that."

"Oh, you mean the loving you part?" I whispered.

"Yes that." He grinned, his eyes shining.

"Well, yeah," I admitted lamely. "Of course I do," I added quietly. As scary as it was, it felt good to say it out loud, like a weight was lifted off my shoulders.

"Were you thinkin' of sharin' that anytime soon?" he asked with a raised brow.

"I just did," I defended.

"A slip of the tongue doesn't count." He chuckled,

moving us backward toward the bed.

"What are you doing? I have to get ready for work," I protested as his lips found my neck and made my knees quake. I was quickly losing my will power.

"Already told you, you're off the schedule for tonight. Now, you just told me you love me and I'm going to take you to bed to show my appreciation," he told me, his voice low and full of promise against my skin.

"You are so bossy," I grumbled, though the fight had clearly gone out of me.

"Yeah, but you love it," he smiled as his body landed on top of mine.

He was right of course, but there was no way I was admitting it.

Chapter Twelve

The next few weeks passed with very little drama. I wasn't thrown from any moving vehicles or kidnapped. My bruises and skin had healed, and I was relieved to look like myself again.

Cole and I found a comfortable rhythm with our living situation. I had to admit that his place had begun to feel more like home, despite the fact that I hadn't unpacked any of my boxes. I knew it was largely due to my stubbornness, but I also wanted a chance for us to settle into something that felt like normalcy before I took that plunge. The only minor flare-ups that erupted involved my work schedule. Cole really didn't like when I worked the late shift, but I was adamant. He'd already paid one month's worth of my bills and that wasn't happening again. So one of the guys took me to work and picked me up when Cole wasn't available. Other than that, I loved being under the same roof as Cole. I loved coming home to him and having him come home to me. It felt natural, and I was happier than I'd ever been in my life. I was trying not to let that scare the crap out of me.

I heard the garage door and the rumble of Cole's Harley as I put the groceries away that I just bought. It was Friday evening and Wes had been nice enough to take me to the store so I could cook dinner for Cole and me. I hated relying on someone to take me places, but the guys had all been so generous and patient about it.

"Hi, babe," he greeted, kissing my neck as I put away a six pack in the fridge.

"Hi. I thought I'd cook dinner." I smiled up at him.

"Sounds good. I'm starved," he said while grabbing a beer. I watched his eyes sweep the room, eyeing my unpacked boxes without comment as he did every evening. I knew it bothered him that I hadn't unpacked, but he hadn't brought it up. "Who took you to the store?" he asked, his eyes returning to me.

"Wes," I answered as I put a pot of water on to boil.

He nodded without comment, his gaze returning to my boxes.

"He's having some people over later – want to head over there after dinner?" I asked hopefully. I was in the mood to let loose after feeling a bit like a caged animal all week.

"Alright," he agreed.

He sat with me while I whipped up some pasta, garlic bread, and salad. Nothing fancy, but he seemed to appreciate every meal I made.

"Pop took another meet with the Sinners," he shared after we dug in.

"Oh?" I asked curiously. There hadn't been any news on Jake or Victor but that wasn't for lack of effort. I knew Cole and the boys were spending a majority of their time hunting. It worried me, especially when Cole was gone late into the night. But Cole was not the type of man you could voice concern over. He had his pride and I respected that.

"The only good to come out of this shit is that it brought the clubs back together. We have the same agenda and priority, to bring those mother fuckers down. You have our protection and theirs as well. Not that I'd let any of those boys take direct responsibility for you," he shared. "Years back it was far more beneficial for both clubs to work together so once this storm has passed, I see good things," he added, taking a swig of beer.

"Did they vote in the new prez?" I asked. Cole had gotten word that the Sinners would be voting any day now.

"Yep, it's Henry," he said as he grinned.

I grinned back, they couldn't have picked better. "Finally someone deserving of the title," I sighed, feeling a relief that surprised me. "My dad would love that," I added quietly.

Cole reached over and took my hand in a brief squeeze.

"I wish you could have met him. He would have loved you," I said, meeting his gaze.

"Me too, babe," he agreed while giving me another squeeze before returning to his meal. That was his way of giving me a second with my thoughts and I loved him for it.

Later that night Connie, Ettie, Kat, and I were hanging out in Wes's backyard drinking beers. I felt utterly content to be with my girlfriends and to watch my man from across the fire pit. He stood talking with Sal, his gaze sweeping over to me every few minutes. My stomach pitched every time our gaze met. I wondered if he'd always have such a powerful effect on me, though I felt pretty confident that he would. When he looked at me with that blue-eyed, intense stare, I felt like we were the only two people in the world.

"You have it bad," Connie said as she giggled and I

tore my eyes from Cole and blushed.

"Yeah, I do," I admitted shamelessly.

"You're no better," I teased, throwing my bottle cap at her. She and Wes were constantly affectionate – it was almost nauseating.

"I know, I know," she said as she laughed.

"I wish Sal was more affectionate in public," Kat grumbled. It had been one of the points of contention between them.

"Have you seen the way he looks at you?" I asked her with a reassuring smile. "He may not be overly affectionate around us, but no one would doubt the way he feels," I assured her.

"True," Connie backed me up with a smile.

We grinned at each other just as gunshots rang through the night air. It was as though time stopped when I saw Cole, Wes, Mack, and Sal rush to us as screams and chaos broke out around us. Cole's hard body hit me like a truck as he threw me to the ground and covered me with his body. I was collected enough to see that the other guys were doing the same. Even in my panicked state, I registered how lucky we were to have such loyal, protective men. It was seconds after the blasts stopped that Cole heaved me up and pulled me to the house almost roughly, shielding me with his body the entire time. He looked me over, his eyes sweeping my body to make sure I was okay before his eyes turned with fury toward the street.

"Mack's hit," Sal informed us harshly, looking nearly as pissed off as Cole did. All the men were seething at the blatant attack on the club and its women.

"Motherfucker. How bad?" Cole demanded.

"Shoulder, not life threatening. Got hit shielding Ettie.

Better him than her. Hank's coming to take him to the ER once we give the all clear," he said, his eyes glimmering with anger.

"Good," Cole said, pulling his phone out and in a few short words, delivering the news to his father.

He hung up and turned to me. "You okay?" he asked, his tone harsh. This was not a time for soft assurances.

I managed to nod.

"Stay here," he ordered.

"What? You're leaving?" I asked incredulously.

"Wes, Tag, Xander: you're with me," he ordered instead of answering me. "Sal, Axel: stay with the women," he barked, his anger palpable.

My body was shaking from the shock of being shot at. The fact that Cole was leaving to head directly into the source of danger did nothing for my nerves.

Cole turned to me and stooped slightly to meet my eyes, his hands cupping the sides of my face. "Stay here, listen to Sal. Once all's clear, someone will take you home if I'm not able to."

A calm resolve came over me as I nodded. I knew with crushing clarity that he needed me to be strong and to accept his directive with no question. If I was going to stand beside him as I wanted to with all my heart, than at times like this I needed to be a source of strength for him rather than a drain on his reserves.

Wes stalked over and grabbed the back of my neck with surprising force. "Take care of Connie, okay?" We both looked over and it was clear that Connie was falling to pieces. "You're not even shakin'," he muttered. It was obvious that the last thing he wanted to do was leave. Giving me the responsibility of taking care of her wasn't done lightly, and I didn't take it for granted.

"I promise," I nodded, meeting his fierce gaze. Kat looked better than Connie but not by much. It was clear that I needed to step it up and I fell into my role with ease.

I gave Cole an assuring look to let him now I had it under control, and I walked off toward my girls offering beers and a promise of a rom-com marathon.

"She's got this," I heard Wes rumble with confidence as they grabbed their jackets and made a rapid exit.

"She does," I heard Cole reply as they strode out the door, his tone filled with fierce adoration and a confidence that I was determined not to betray.

After two movies and more chocolate ice cream than beers, the three of us started to drift off. Sal and Axel had taken their job as protectors extremely seriously and they stayed discretely armed and took frequent laps of the small property. Sal had shown an unusual amount of affection toward Kat, clearly worried about her. When he wasn't walking the property or talking on the phone outside of hearing range, he had an arm around his girl. Despite the evening's events, I was glad to see it.

"Scarlet," a deep voice rumbled, waking me from my uncomfortable slumber on the leather couch. "Time to go home."

I woke up and groggily peered up to see Wes hunched down over me. "Where's Cole?" I asked, my voice raspy with sleep.

"He'll be a little while longer," he answered, and I knew he didn't plan to elaborate. I also knew not to ask any more questions and I rose silently to follow him to his bike.

"Connie's okay," I told him quietly when we'd parked at the curb in front of Cole's house.

"Thank you," he answered gruffly. Despite his rough demeanor, his gratitude was undoubtedly sincere.

I'd grown to really like Wes.

He did a very thorough walk-through of Cole's place before gesturing for me to go inside. It occurred to me that I wished we had a guard dog at times like this so I wouldn't have to be alone. But in the end, I was too tired to be worried and I fell into a deep sleep soon after Wes left the house to park himself out front until Cole got home.

What felt like minutes later, but could have been hours, I woke up to tingles shooting straight to my toes and an arch in my back. Cole was settled between my legs and I moaned, coming fully awake as his tongue worked magic at my core. He brought me nearly to the brink before he moved up and sank fully inside of me.

"Cole," I breathed as he pulled out and glided back in. This wasn't his typical punishing rhythm. It was slow and sweet. "Love you, Cole," I moaned, feeling the momentum build inside of me.

He kissed my neck and brought his lips to my ear. "Unpack, babe," his voice was low and full of promise.

"Cole…." my voice trailed off.

"Life's too short, babe. Unpack," he demanded, holding himself still inside of me when I desperately wanted him to move. "And I'm not talking about for a few weeks. I'm talking permanently," he added.

"This is sexual coercion," I argued breathlessly.

He reared up, his arms braced at either side of my head. His eyes glimmered with intensity as they stared down into mine. "Scarlet, I love you. I want us to share a roof. Unpack," he said again.

"Okay," I agreed finally. There just wasn't any arguing

with him, not that I truly wanted to anyway.

"Okay," he whispered, pressing his lips to mine. I didn't know what happened that night, but something sinister had transpired. I could see it in his face and in his clear need to keep me close. He began to move once more, this time faster and with more determination. It wasn't long before we were both moaning out our release.

He rolled off of me, but pulled me close into the crook of his arm. "You can't take it back you know," he pointed out, his tone mildly teasing.

I laughed softly. "I don't want to," I said as I shook my head, feeling satiated and relieved he was home safe. "I was wondering though…." I trailed off.

"What?" he asked.

"Can we maybe get a dog? I was thinking tonight that it would have been nice to have a guard dog or something," I told him while biting my lip. "More for company than anything else," I mumbled. Before I could stop myself, I continued. "And it would have to be a dog that would be good with kids too… you know, just in case we, you know, someday." I was rambling now.

"Yeah, we can do that babe." He squeezed me, his tone surprisingly pleasing.

"Is Mack okay?" I asked worriedly.

"He's fine," he assured me. "Just a flesh wound. He'll be released tomorrow."

"You okay?" I asked quietly.

"Yeah, babe. But I'm wiped, let's get some sleep," he replied, not welcoming further conversation. I'd let him have that for now. I didn't want to push him and I trusted him to tell me what I needed to know, while sparing me the details of what I might not.

Chapter Thirteen

I slipped soundlessly out of bed the next morning, leaving Cole deeply asleep. I made coffee and started to unpack a few of my kitchen boxes. I knew it would please Cole, and truth be told I was ready to have my things intermingled with his. I was nearly done when he emerged wearing only his boxers. I'd never tire of looking at his body, his sculpted chest and stomach. He reminded me of a lion with his lithe physique that held a promise of shear power underneath its grace. His beautiful eyes swept over me and they grew warm when he saw what I was doing.

"Coffee?" I offered.

"Yeah, coffee would be good," he said with a small smile on his lips. I'd totally been caught ogling him.

I rolled my eyes at him and handed him his cup.

I let him drink his coffee as I whipped up some pancakes and bacon. It wasn't until he'd eaten half of it that I looked at him expectantly from my place in front of the stove.

"Victor's dead." He answered my unspoken question with brutal honestly.

I had promised myself that I'd be calm despite anything he might tell me, and hoped that I successfully kept my face clear of the shock that his admission sent through me.

"How?" I asked simply, leaning a hip against the counter.

He sighed. "Do you really want to know? I'll tell you if you do," he answered, his eyes piercing mine.

Did I really want to know? I thought about it for a few beats before I shook my head. "No, I don't want to know," I answered him. "And Jake?" I asked.

"In the wind," he answered, sounding aggravated.

"Henry made Benny his new lieutenant. Do you know him?" he asked me as he shoveled the last of his breakfast in his mouth.

"Yeah, I know Benny," I answered quietly.

Benny had always been kind to me in a gruff sort of way. He was older than me – mid 40s with a tough old lady named Darla. He'd always been loyal to my father and I wasn't surprised that Henry had chosen him.

"He's in town for a while, his chief directive from Henry is to take Jake down. He rode out with us last night," he explained.

"Is Jake working alone at this point or does he still have help?" I asked while taking a much needed sip of my coffee.

The fact that Victor had been killed by someone close to me, maybe even by Cole, had me rattled. I didn't like the fact that my past was forcing blood to be spilled. Even after everything Victor had done to me, it didn't sit comfortably that he died more or less because of me.

"Seems to be alone, especially after what went down

last night. No one would be stupid enough to partner with that crazy motherfucker at this point," Cole grumbled.

I nodded in full agreement. "Victor was the brains behind the operation. Jake is just crazy." I sighed. "I don't know if that makes me feel safer or not," I mused.

"He won't fucking touch you," Cole growled.

"I know, babe," I assured him. "Is Henry coming back into town? I should cook him up some of my ribs. Benny, too." I said, in need of a subject change. Now that the relationship had improved between the clubs, I was anxious to do my part to encourage that however I could.

Cole's eyebrows rose and I was gratified to see his mood lighten. "You been holdin' out on me?"

I blushed slightly. "Not intentionally. I don't make them often. But Henry loves them," I said.

"Pop's been talking about having a barbecue for both clubs. I'll ask him about it," he told me as he rose from his seat to put his plate in the dishwasher. He came to stand behind me, put his arms around my belly and kissed my neck. "He also mentioned that he still has the photos of your dad to show you."

"Yeah, I'd like that," I murmured. With all the craziness of the last few weeks, I hadn't had the chance to sit down with Cal for a trip down memory lane. Part of me was probably avoiding it to some extent. There was only so much emotional baggage I could strap on at one time.

"Glad you're movin' in, babe," he murmured in my ear, creating tingles down my spine.

"Yeah, me too." I molded my body to his. "I need to tell Kat. I feel a little guilty, I don't want to leave her in the lurch," I muttered.

"She's never there anyway, is she? Every time I go to

Sal's place, she's there," Cole replied.

He was right about that. Kat spent the majority of her nights at Sal's place, but she'd still need half of the rent paid. I shared this with Cole.

He shrugged. "If she's never there than it shouldn't matter much who it is."

"Yeah, but she's not entirely sure how solid things are with Sal," I informed him before I could stop myself.

"What? Why not?" he asked, surprised.

I shrugged. "He's just not that affectionate or vocal about his feelings toward her," I shared.

"That's just Sal," Cole waved his hand dismissively. "Trust me. He's a goner."

"I'm glad to hear it, but he could probably work on making that more clear to Kat," I said. "He could learn a few tricks from you," I said and smiled suggestively.

Cole chuckled. "Sorry, babe. I'm not having a talk with Sal about his love life. Not gonna happen."

"Dammit," I muttered, knowing he'd say as much.

"I gotta head to the club, check in with Pop. What's your schedule?" he asked. I realized this was something he'd always want to know regardless of my safety. It was just how he operated.

"Unpacking, gym, hospital, and work," I answered simply.

"Hospital?" he asked with a creased brow.

"Yeah, gotta see Mack," I answered with a shrug.

I saw Cole's eyes warm until they were liquid. "I didn't tell you how well you handled yourself last night. I was proud," he said seriously.

I shrugged again, feigning indifference, though his words thrilled me. "No use falling apart over things you can't control. I learned that a long time ago."

"Now's not the time to discuss it, but if I did decide to fill my father's shoes, it's nice to know my woman can handle the job that comes with that," he told me, his eyes full of pride and love.

I stood on my tiptoes and kissed him, watching as he gathered his things to head out for the day. I had never thought I'd want to be back in the life, but with a man like Cole I'd want to do just about anything.

"And babe, shit obviously got stepped up last night. I don't want to argue, but we need to have a serious talk about your work schedule until this shit blows over. Working the late shift puts you and my guys on the line," he said firmly.

"I'll talk to Pete today," I promised without delay.

My instant compliance clearly surprised him and his eyebrows rose. I rolled my eyes. "Of course I don't want to put anyone in danger, Cole. I'll just work the day shift for now."

He kissed my forehead tenderly. "Thanks, babe."

I started unpacking my things as soon as Cole left. Despite my earlier reservations, now that I'd agreed I was anxious to do so. I started in the kitchen, moved to the bedroom, and finished in the bathroom. I was just thinking how quickly I'd completed the job when I unearthed a box of tampons from one of the boxes. My heart immediately stopped beating and then started back up again, double time. How long had it been since I needed those? I knew the answer – too long. With everything that had been going on, I hadn't been keeping track. I didn't even notice that I missed a period.

It's not possible, I told myself. I was religious about taking my pills. Except for maybe my stay in the hospital, and maybe when I went to Idaho... and Connie's place. Fuck!

I called Kat immediately, my hands shaking as I held the phone to my ear. "I need you to bring a pregnancy test over here, now," I told her without a hello or a greeting of any kind.

"Be there in ten," she answered without question. See, this is why she was my best friend.

Twenty minutes later we were sitting on my new bathroom counter watching the little blue stick create two blue lines.

"No," I breathed feeling like I might pass out.

"Let's take another one, I bought like five of them," she suggested, her tone calm, though I could tell she was far from it.

I nodded woodenly.

Now we were staring at three different pregnancy tests all in various states of "you are pregnant!" Did I really need the digital version and the lines to confirm it? Really, it was just like throwing it in my face at that point.

"Shit," I said, dumbfounded as we continued to stare at the tests.

"Yeah," she agreed. There wasn't much else to say at the moment.

"What are you going to do?" she asked quietly.

"I'm going to stare at them for about ten more minutes," I answered through barely-moving lips.

"Okay," she agreed instantly.

I finally pulled myself together and we left the bathroom to go sit on the couch in the living room.

"Well, let's get you in to see the doctor," Kat stated. I so appreciated her taking control in this moment because I was completely unable to. I was still reeling from the shock of my life. I didn't feel pregnant. Weren't you supposed to be throwing up or something? I just felt like me, sans period.

My OB could fit me in that day, in just an hour, so we continued to sit on the couch talking about the possibilities.

"Would you keep it?" she asked tentatively.

"Yeah," I answered without hesitation.

"How do you think Cole will feel when you tell him?"

"I have absolutely no idea," I answered truthfully. "We've been together three months, if that," I added with a bit of panic in my voice.

"Well, we'll just cross that bridge," she assured me.

"Yeah, well, for now you're steering, because I have absolutely no idea what I'm doing," I admitted.

"Deal," she agreed.

Like a best friend would, she drove me to my appointment. Hank had tailed us but we hadn't given him any details other than it being a "lady doctor" appointment. Unsurprisingly, after that, he didn't ask for more details. It would have been comical if I wasn't so freaked out. Kat came in with me as the doctor confirmed that I was indeed pregnant, though very early on.

"I see you were on several different antibiotics," he noted while reviewing my chart.

"Yeah," I nodded. They'd been prescribed after my not so little brush with the concrete via one Victor-Friggin-Cross.

"They told you that could interfere with your birth control?" he asked.

Well, if I'd allowed them to check me out, they probably would have.

"I wasn't aware of that," I answered evasively. "But I skipped a few pills as well," I admitted.

"It was probably more likely to be the medication unless you missed a lot of pills," he told me.

Well, at least it wasn't all my fault. That didn't really help my current freak out that I was suddenly six weeks pregnant.

"What the fuck am I going to do?" I lamented as we sat parked in front of my new home. The home I had just moved into with my brand new boyfriend. God, this was bad. Very, very bad.

"You're going to tell the guy who loves you that you're going to have his baby, a bit earlier than expected," she answered.

The prospect of telling Cole felt so surreal, I couldn't even get my head around it.

"This would have happened anyway Scar, you two are made for each other. You're just a bit ahead of schedule," she soothed.

"Yeah, like years ahead," I scoffed.

She patted my leg sympathetically. "I get to be an auntie." She let out her first small burst of excitement at the news.

I grinned despite myself. "Yeah, you do."

"He or she is going to be so freaking cute, I mean, look at you two!" she exclaimed.

I allowed myself to picture it for the first time, though it still hadn't truly sunk in. "Yeah, we'll make a beautiful baby," I sighed.

"The most beautiful," she emphasized.

I smiled at her. "Thank you. As always, you're the best."

"You'd do the same for me," she said.

"I would," I agreed.

"When are you going to tell him?" she wanted to know.

"No idea."

"Well, my lips are sealed," she promised while making the motion.

"They'd better be." I laughed dryly. "I might not tell him until this kid is in college.

Chapter Fourteen

By midnight that night, I was nearing the end of my shift and I was exhausted. I couldn't stop thinking about being pregnant. It would certainly take a while for that to really settle in.

It was a particularly busy Saturday night. The one saving grace was that my conversation with Pete had gone well and there'd be no problem keeping me off of night shifts. All the other servers wanted them because the tips were the best late at night. I'd just have to tighten my purse strings for a while, a better choice than having someone get hurt so I can make some extra cash.

The large table of fraternity boys wasn't helping my night end any faster. They'd become rowdier with every round, and I was in no mood for the lewd comments they'd started to spew every time I was forced to check on their table. Unfortunately, it came with the territory, but nights like this made me seriously ponder another line of work.

"Hey baby, bring that sweet ass back over here!" one of the guys hollered breaking my reverie.

I could hear the want ads on craigslist calling my name.

"You want me to switch with you?" Connie asked, coming up behind me and eyeing the table with disdain.

I shook my head. "No, but thanks. We've all had tables like this. It's my cross to bear." I sighed dramatically, making her laugh.

"Better tell them to keep a lid on it. Sal is getting pissed," she shared. I looked over and Sal, my ride home for the evening, was indeed seething. All the guys took their job of looking out for me extremely seriously. Anyone fucking with me was a slight on the Knights, with or without the Jake mess.

"Okay, I'll do my best," I nodded.

I walked over and looked at the table expectantly. "What can I get you?" I asked, my tone clipped.

"Another round and your phone number," the loudest of the group of five boomed.

"Sorry, spoken for. Same as last time?" I asked, indicating toward the pitcher. This would be their last round. I'd ask the bar to cut them off after this.

"How about a quickie in the back then?" he persisted before reaching around and squeezing my ass.

"Hey!" I heard a very familiar voice bark from behind me. "Get your fucking hands off!" Cole growled as he stood next to me, putting my body behind his. He cast a formidable presence as he glowered down at the group. I wasn't expecting him and I figured Sal had probably called him. Great.

The group looked up at him belligerently, but Mr. Grab Hands had the audacity to sneer. Cole didn't miss it and he didn't like it either. "That was your last drink," he commanded, nodding toward the empty glasses. "Settle up and get the fuck out. And if you stiff her, we've got problems," he added.

"Oh I'll give her a stiff one alright," one of them

snorted.

I rolled my eyes, so the wrong thing to say.

"What did you just say?" Cole demanded, his tone full of such menace that even I was afraid.

"Nothing man," the smartest one of the bunch spoke up. "We were just leaving," he added while looking meaningfully at his friends.

Loud guy scoffed. "I'm not going to let roughneck kick me out. Sweet cheeks here was just getting us another round," he indicated toward me.

Oh shit.

"Cole, I need this job," I whispered quietly, knowing that if he caused a big enough scene I'd lose it.

He turned to me with fire in his eyes. "You'd rather let him disrespect you and, in doing so, disrespect me?" he demanded. "You don't need this fucking job that bad," he added and I bit my lower lip. He was really pissed off. I noted to myself that interrupting him at times like this was probably ill advised. We were still getting to know each other, but I knew Cole well enough to know when I needed to let him do things his way. Now was one of those times.

I simply nodded, backed off, and stood next to Connie.

"Get up. All of you," Cole barked to the group.

"You gonna take us all on, tough guy?" Grab Hands asked incredulously.

"It would be my fucking pleasure preppy, but I'd hate to ruin the fun for my friends," Cole glowered just as Wes and Sal appeared as if on cue to stand behind him. The three of them cut a menacing picture and despite the odds being five against three, I could see one or two of the frat guys visibly gulp.

"Outside," Cole repeated, his voice so low I could

barely hear him.

The group rose hesitantly and I made a mental bet that they'd high tail it the second they got outside. Cole, Sal, and Wes followed them out and I sighed, exasperated. "I wish Sal would have kept that information to himself," I grumbled.

Connie patted me sympathetically as they disappeared from sight. "Cole would have his head if something happened and he didn't at least give him the option to take care of it," she informed me.

"Such macho idiots," I continued to grumble.

"Yeah, but they're our macho idiots," she said as she laughed, linking arms with me.

I was just finishing cashing out when Cole stalked back in and scanned the room until his eyes found mine. His chest was heaving and anger still flared on his face. Despite complaining about his antics, the fact that he was always so intent on protecting me turned me on. I walked up to him slowly and his eyes tracked every step as I got nearer. When I reached him, I put my hands on his chest before moving my arms up to link behind is neck. His expression visibly shifted as he caught my mood.

"You ready to go home?" I asked, softly meeting his fiery gaze.

"Yeah, baby," he rumbled, his hands moving to my ass and lifting me so that my legs wrapped around his waist. I was too turned on by the gesture to be embarrassed by the catcalls from our friends, as he strode out of the place with me wrapped around him.

We barely made it through the door before we were all over each other. He had me pressed firmly against the wall in the hallway that led to the bedroom as I panted into his mouth. I loved how strong he was, how he could lift me and hold me any way he chose.

"You want it right here?" he growled into my mouth, his muscles flexing under my fingers.

"Yeah," I replied breathlessly. I could feel his hardness through his jeans and a thrill went through me as he pressed himself into me. He dropped me to the ground long enough to strip me out of my jeans and underwear. He pressed me back against the wall as his fingers glided through my slick folds.

"Soaked," he rumbled with pleasure as he unzipped his jeans to give him access. There was something undeniably erotic and utterly primal about him being fully dressed. He hoisted me back up and plunged into me. I threw my head back and cried out loudly as he immediately started hitting the spot I needed him to.

Wall sex was a new one for us, and I knew immediately that I'd be demanding a repeat performance.

My hands clutched at his shoulders as he slammed into me. There was a desperation about his movements that I hadn't seen before, but I welcomed it. My intensity stemmed from a different source entirely, one I wouldn't be sharing with him tonight. For now I just needed to feel connected to him.

"Oh, babe," I moaned when I felt it coming like a freight train. Seconds later I was quaking around him, my legs wrapping even tighter around his firm ass to pull him deeper. He groaned and thrust two more times before he was following me over the edge.

"Fuck," he breathed into my neck as he still held me pressed to the wall.

"Yeah," I agreed simply, my voice a hoarse whisper.

"Let's do that again." I smiled while kissing his neck.

"Think I need a quick breather, babe," he chuckled.

"Well, I didn't mean now," I replied, blushing slightly.

He set me on my feet and tucked himself back into his jeans. He kissed me softly before biting my lower lip lightly. "Love how you get so wild for me, but you still blush like a schoolgirl," he said as he grinned.

I swatted him away playfully as he took my hand and dragged me toward the shower.

"I've got a surprise for you," he told me later as I lay sprawled against his chest.

My heart hammered with the knowledge that I had a very large surprise for him as well. And I wasn't sure at all how he would react. I still wasn't even sure how I felt about it.

We'd just finished round two, which had been Cole's chance to play. I felt utterly satiated after hours of giving my body over to his knowing hands, so luckily I was able to fall back into relaxation mode rather easily. His fingers traced patterns over my shoulder and I hummed with pleasure.

"What kind of surprise?" I asked.

He chuckled. "It wouldn't be a surprise if I told you, now would it?"

I pouted. "I suppose not, when can I have it?" I asked, propping myself up on my elbow to look at him in wide-eyed delight. No one had ever gotten me a surprise before and I was excited by the prospect.

"Tomorrow," he answered simply.

Maybe he could have his tomorrow as well, when I figured out how the hell to tell him.

Fortunately, I was too exhausted to think about it too

much before my eyelids grew heavy and I fell asleep.

Chapter Fifteen

The doorbell rang just as I was finishing breakfast. Cole came out of the office and headed for the door, giving me a wink. My surprise, no doubt.

On the other side of the door Wes stood with a huge, ferocious-looking dog. My eyes bulged in response.

"What on earth is that?" I demanded.

"Your new dog," Cole replied as the beast came trotting into the house like he owned it.

"My new dog?" I sputtered. "He looks like he'll kill me, not protect me." I protested, eyeing the dog warily as it came to sniff my leg.

Cole rolled his eyes as Wes let himself in to grab a cup of coffee. "It's a Bullmastiff. They're great family dogs but they also make great guard dogs. My pop knew someone who trains them and it just so happened that Chief here was in need of a new home."

"What, did he eat his old owners?" I demanded as Wes sputtered on his coffee as he held back a laugh.

"Just give him a shot," Cole said as he chuckled. "Maybe someday we can get a cute cuddly little puppy that will piss all over the place. But for now, Chief is already fully trained. You were right that we should have a dog.

It'll make me feel more secure to know he's here with you," Cole explained, trying to appeal to my common sense.

I was momentarily distracted with the realization that we wouldn't have time for a puppy, we'd be too busy changing poopy diapers. Oh boy.

I forced myself not to think about that, and after doing so, I realized I was a bit annoyed by this "surprise." When I'd mentioned getting a dog, I envisioned something a little less huge. I'd also pictured us picking it out together, but now wasn't the time for that conversation, not in front of Wes.

I continued to watch the dog as he padded around the house, his large nails clicking on the hardwood. He was beautiful in a ferocious kind of way, with a shiny brindle coat and a large square head. He quickly completed his perusal of the house and settled comfortably on the carpet in the living room.

"Sure didn't take much time for him to make himself at home," I muttered.

"You'll love him, you'll see," Cole told me, kissing my head reassuringly. "Wes and I have some shit to take care of. It will give you two time to bond," he added.

"Sure," I snorted.

Both men chuckled at my sarcasm as they headed out after setting the alarm. The house was suddenly quiet after the roar of Cole's truck had disappeared.

"Well, just you and me, huh?" I asked Chief, feeling suddenly idiotic for talking to a dog. I'd never had one before. I'd always wanted one, but I could never quite convince my dad that it was a good idea. Chief cocked his head at me as though he wanted to answer my question. I laughed out loud. I had to admit he was pretty cute.

"I guess the test to see if you're a good family dog is going to come a little sooner than I'd intended," I continued to babble to him. "That is, if Cole doesn't go running for the hills," I continued. Chief just watched me with warm brown eyes. "No advice, huh?" I asked him. "Didn't think so," I sighed.

After a few hours of having a new and very large shadow, I had to admit that Chief had grown on me. He had such an expressive face and such human looking big brown eyes. He followed me everywhere in the house, even lying in the bathroom while I showered.

"Shit, that's a big dog!" Kat exclaimed, comically taking a step back in surprise. She'd come over for girl talk that was being disguised as mani-pedis. The guys were still taking care of "shit," and Kat and I had learned how to use that time wisely.

"I know, he's sweet though," I assured her, patting Chief's head affectionately.

"Is 'kill' one of his known commands?" she asked dryly as we settled onto the couch.

"Maybe." I laughed. Truth be told, I had no idea what he was actually trained to do.

"Still haven't told him yet, huh?" she asked quietly.

"Nope," I replied, my lips popping on the "p" for emphasis.

"Why not?"

I sighed. "Because I'm terrified that he'll think I did it on purpose. I'm scared he'll take off because of it. Or worse yet, that he'll think he has to stay because of it." I grimaced.

"Honey, you gotta tell him," she said softly.

"I know, I will. So, how's the roommate search going?"

I asked not only because I wanted to know, but also because I wanted to change the subject.

She shrugged. "Okay, I guess. Honestly, I haven't been trying very hard to find someone," she admitted.

"How are you going to pay the rent?" I asked, clearly confused.

She blushed a little and my eyes narrowed. I knew a guilty face when I saw one. "Spill," I demanded simply.

"I promised I wouldn't," she said meekly.

"Spill," I demanded again.

She sighed in resignation. "Fine, but you can't get mad. It was super nice of him."

"Nice of who?" I asked suspiciously.

"Well, Cole sort of um, paid your half of the rent for three months," she confided.

"He what?" I exclaimed.

She shrugged. "He didn't want me to have to worry about it. And I think he knew that if I was worried that you'd be less likely to shack up with him."

"Sneaky bastard," I mumbled. "It was kind of him to do that," I admitted. "But I'm still far from comfortable with the extent that he wants to take care of me financially, and I'm starting to have an issue with how many decisions he makes without my input," I sighed exasperated. "He just kind of railroads me into things. Granted, he ends up being right most of the time, but that's not the point," I ranted.

"You should talk to him about it. I think you're also probably feeling particularly vulnerable at the moment with what's going on, too," she said. She was probably right about that.

"What's the latest with our friend Sal?" I asked with a

raised brow.

"Same ole same ole," she said sadly. "I'm in love with someone who is so closed off, it's a wonder I'm able to get anything out of him," she told me, looking out the window forlornly. "I don't know Scar, something is going to have to give. I know everyone says he's never been like this before with anyone... blah, blah. But it's still not enough. I don't think I'm asking for too much, but it may be too much for him."

I reached out to squeeze her hand. "What exactly is it that you feel like you're not getting?"

"It's hard to explain. Intimacy? I guess that would be the best way to describe it. Of course we have physical intimacy in spades, but I'm talking about more emotional stuff. He doesn't share. He doesn't communicate very well. I know that he cares about me, but I have to read between the lines," she huffed and I was shocked to see her eyes fill up with tears. This situation was far worse than I'd thought. "I've never felt this way about anyone, but I feel like sometimes even when I'm with him I'm on an island all alone," she sniffed.

"Oh sweetie, I'm sorry," I said softly. I didn't know what else to say. We'd talked about Sal until our faces turned blue. But we couldn't change how he was. She either had to accept it or move on.

"Yeah, well, we'll just have to see. Enough of that," she said as she tried to laugh, waving her hand as though to dismiss the subject.

When Cole got home it was late into the evening and Kat was just on her way out.

"See ya, Cole. Nice horse you've got there." She laughed and cocked her head toward Chief who had joined in our festivities and had quickly charmed her.

Cole just chuckled and lifted his chin toward her as she headed out the front door.

"Hi, babe." I smiled and got up to greet him with a soft kiss.

"Hey," he replied, his fingers trailing through my hair and grasping the back of my neck. This was how Cole almost always greeted me and I loved it. "How'd you two get along?" he asked as he reached down to pet Chief.

"Me and the dog or me and Kat?" I teased.

He rolled his eyes. "You and the dog, babe."

"He's sweet," I admitted. "We got along just fine. Did you eat?" I asked, opening the fridge to peruse its contents.

I was surprised when he closed the door on me. "You gonna thank me, babe?" he asked suggestively. I knew he was only teasing, but based on what I'd shared with Kat earlier the implication pissed me off.

"I would have if you included me in the decision," I replied somewhat curtly.

His brows shot up, my response had clearly surprised him. "What?"

I sighed and leaned against the fridge door with my arms crossed over my chest. "I appreciate the gesture. I appreciate all of your gestures, but we're living together now. If this is really going to go somewhere, then you can't continue to make decisions for me," I explained. "We need to make decisions together."

"Like what?" he demanded, clearly unhappy with this line of discussion.

"Like the dog. He's great but I've never had a dog before. I've wanted one my whole life. I would have loved to look online, to be a part of the process," I explained.

"And like paying for my apartment for months without talking to me about it. That's not something you just do behind my back."

"Behind your back?" he replied curtly. "Jesus that's a bit dramatic, don't you think?" he demanded, leaning against the opposite counter and regarding me with narrowed eyes.

"Did you intend to tell me about it?" I countered.

He regarded me in silence.

"I'll take that silence as a 'no,' which is exactly my point. Look, I don't want to fight. I wanted to talk calmly about this, something we don't seem very capable of doing," I sighed wearily. "But you didn't shack up with some house mouse, Cole. I'm not going to just go along with every decision you make. That said, I also understand that you have a controlling nature," I said with a raised brow. "What I'm trying to tell you is that there's a limit to how much I'm willing to be controlled," I explained. "You want a strong woman that can stand by your side, then this is what you get," I told him firmly.

We regarded each other for a few moments. All the anger had gone out of me, but I wasn't so sure about him. "Okay," he said finally, his tone considerably calmer.

"Okay?" I asked skeptically.

"You're right." He shrugged, though I could tell it wasn't easy for him to say. "I don't want some doormat. I like that you have an opinion, even when it means you're a pain in my ass," he said as he smirked. "So, I'll work on talking to you about shit before I make decisions, okay? I can't promise it'll be about everything, but I'll work on it."

I nodded. It wasn't like I was expecting a miracle.

I felt like we'd just overcome a huge hurdle in our

relationship with this conversation. Not only because we solved a problem by talking things out, but also because we understood each other. I walked the two paces to him and wrapped my arms around his waist, looking up at him with a smile. "Thanks, babe."

"Yeah," he nodded simply. I could tell it cost him a bit to admit fault, no matter how roundabout of a way he'd done it. "I gotta admit though, I'm confused. Do you want the dog or not?" he asked with a wrinkled brow.

I grinned. "I want the dog."

Chapter Sixteen

The next few days were busy. Cole and I kept missing each other since I was working days and he was busy at night with club business. There just hadn't been a good time to tell him about the baby. Admittedly, I could have probably found the time, but I was nervous about it and wanted the timing to be right. I knew it would come completely out of left field to him. Hell, it had shocked the shit out of me. It was unfair to keep it from him, but I just wasn't ready to tell him yet.

I also hadn't shared with Cole what Kat told me about her and Sal. I knew Cole didn't want to be in the middle of her relationship drama. And at the end of the day, he couldn't do anything to change the way his friend behaved. But I knew she was struggling and I wanted to support her, so I spent a lot of my evenings with her, longing for the cocktails that I couldn't have anymore.

I collapsed in bed on Thursday night after a ten hour day on my feet. I'd been working longer shifts to try to make up for missing out on the night shifts. It wasn't working, but I'd never tell Cole that. Cole was at a meet with his pop, Benny, and Henry. Friday night we'd planned a big get-together with both clubs and yes, my ribs. Now that the negative elements of my old club life had been removed, I was excited to see the guys and their old ladies.

I was just drifting off when Chief started to growl. That was the first I'd ever heard him exhibit such behavior, and my hackles rose along with his.

"What is it?" I asked him stupidly, as though he'd respond. Axel was supposed to be posted out front and I jumped for my phone to call him. No answer. Shit.

Chief continued to growl and I called Cole. No answer. Double shit. I'd set the alarm, I knew I had, but of course I started to question myself. I called Kat, and thankfully she at least picked up.

"Chief is acting really weird. He's growling and I can't get a hold of anyone." I whispered.

"Shit!" she exclaimed. "Sal's with Cole," she told me unnecessarily. Almost all the guys were in that meeting, except for Axel.

I went with my intuition. "I think you better go get Cole, something's wrong," I told her.

"Done," she answered without question. Gotta love my girl.

I sat in the dark bedroom, hearing nothing but my heart pounding out of my chest and Chief restlessly pacing and growling. Should I call the police? It would bring so many questions up if I did that. What if it was just a false alarm? All of a sudden, the bedroom door burst open and Jake stood wild eyed and huge, towering in the doorway. Well, too late to call the police, anyway… and what the hell had happened to the alarm?

"You have got to be fucking joking!" I exclaimed, surprised by my anger. I was so sick of this nutcase jerking me around.

"When the cat's away…" he leered suggestively.

"Do you seriously want to die?" I demanded. "That must be it," I bit out, clutching the bed sheets around myself. I wasn't wearing anything terribly revealing, but I didn't want him to see any part of my skin if I could help it.

Chief was barking now and growling loudly, practically frothing at the mouth. He looked now like the ferocious dog I had first thought him to be, and I was glad for it. Jake hadn't been expecting a dog and was clearly a bit more hesitant with a ninety pound snarling monster blocking his path.

"Call the dog off," he demanded.

"Like hell I will," I scoffed. "Get the fuck out of my house."

"I'll shoot him," he threatened.

My blood ran cold. "Don't," I said, hating how much it sounded like a plea. If I showed any weakness with Jake it would be bad news, and I was determined not to give him the satisfaction.

"Call him off," he said again.

"I don't know if I can," I answered honestly. "He's pretty pissed."

"Try." He glared.

"What did you do to Axel? And how'd you get past the alarm?" I asked suddenly. Axel would never just leave me unattended. All the guys took their jobs extremely seriously.

Jake snorted. "That was too easy. That motherfucker was completely distracted reading a magazine. Now he's taking a nice little nap. I took a few classes in security, the alarm was nothing." He shrugged. "Really Rosie, they should have you better protected," he sneered.

"Don't call me that," I said sharply. Only my father or

Henry got to call me that.

"Whatever you say," he said as he laughed.

I mentally calculated what kind of time I had. I had just hung up with Kat and I inwardly cringed at realizing how long it would take her to get all the way to the clubhouse and then for Cole to get here. I was on my own. I had to keep Jake talking. I had questions anyway.

"What happened to my father, Jacob?" I demanded.

His brows rose in amusement. "Oh, so I'm Jacob now?" He laughed. "You really want to know?" he asked as he leaned in the doorway like he owned the place. He looked casually at his fingernails and I hated how familiar the gesture was. He'd always done it when he was considering something. I hated knowing anything intimate about him.

I swallowed. "Yes, I really want to know."

Chief had calmed some, but he had backed his way to the bed and was clearly guarding me while a low growl continued to emanate from his throat.

Jake shrugged. "He wouldn't give me you, he wouldn't give me the club, didn't think I was worthy," he sneered.

That's because you aren't. I thought.

"So he had to be removed," he explained callously.

"So you killed him," I stated, surprised I could even say the words.

"Well, technically, his bike did." He grinned.

"You are fucking sick," I hissed. "You killed him and you never had the club, and you'll never have me. It was for nothing. You killed him for nothing!" I shrieked.

"Oh, I'll fucking have you," he swore, advancing into the room. Chief started barking again as Jake tried to get at me, and it looked as though Jake was going for his weapon. It wasn't just me I had to protect anymore, and the thought of him doing anything to injure my unborn child made me that much more determined to protect myself.

Chief didn't hesitate and jumped on him, tearing at his clothes, growling and barking so loudly I could barely think. Jake immediately backpedaled, swearing as Chief went after him. He managed to get past the dog for long enough to haul me into him and drag me out of the room, but I fought for all I was worth, knocking over furniture as we went.

Please don't hurt the baby, please, I mentally pleaded, close to tears.

"Fuck!" he bellowed, trying to get a grasp on me.

"Get out!" I screamed back as we slammed into the bookshelf in the living room. I was struggling for all I was worth. Chief was following trying to get a bite out of Jake. It was utter chaos.

He pulled my hair back painfully. "This isn't over, it'll never be over," he swore to me, kissing my neck wetly. I shivered in revulsion as he let me go and exited abruptly out of the back door.

I don't know how long I stood in the middle of the living room, furniture toppled over and shaking when Cole, Wes, and Sal burst in through the front door. Chief again took guard and stood in front of me barking ferociously at them.

"Fuck!" I heard Cole explode upon seeing me and the obvious state of a struggle. "Babe... Scarlet. You alright?" he demanded over Chief's loud barking.

I managed to nod, still trying to collect myself.

"Call the dog off," Wes commanded.

"I don't know how," I admitted.

"You don't need to command him, just tell him it's okay. Let him know you're okay," Wes told me.

I took in his words and nodded. It took me a minute and a few deep breaths before I knelt down to Chief and wrapped my arms around his large body. "I'm okay buddy. You can calm down now. You did a good job," I murmured. And miraculously, it worked. Chief immediately cooled down and stopped barking. He was still clearly on alert, but he let the guys get further into the room.

"Is Axel alright?" I asked immediately.

Sal nodded. "Knocked on the head pretty good but he'll be okay. He's more upset than anything that he let the fucker sneak up on him."

I nodded, relieved that he was okay.

"What happened?" Cole demanded, clearly seething.

I gave a brief recount of the story and saw three sets of eyes turn black with anger.

"Far as I'm concerned, that dog can have a gold-plated dish," Cole bit out.

"I don't think he'd care too much about that," I answered dumbly. I was still in quite a daze, standing in my living room wearing very little clothing. I was starting to feel a little light headed.

After ascertaining that I wasn't seriously hurt, Sal and Wes took their cue to leave and went to attend to Axel.

Cole came across the room, ignoring Chief's low rumble and took me in his strong arms. "I'm so sorry, babe. I thought you were being looked out for," he choked. The emotion rippled off his body in waves.

I interrupted him by grasping his forearm. "I think I need to lay down or…" I wasn't able to finish the sentence. I must have passed out because the next thing I knew I was laying on the bed with Cole looking down at me worriedly.

"Baby, should we go have you checked out?" he asked,

his eyes bright with concern.

I felt completely rung out and not quite lucid. "Cole," I began, my voice somewhat hoarse. "Honey, I'm pregnant," I told him.

I didn't register his reaction or his expression. All I knew was that he lifted me and carried me to his truck. I didn't ask questions as he deposited me gently in the passenger seat. I just let him take charge as we drove through the night.

He carried me in through the emergency room exit and the next thing I knew, I was hooked up to every machine imaginable. Cole sat vigilant at my side with his large hand over mine.

When the baby's heartbeat echoed loud and overwhelming in its vitality throughout the room, my breath caught. It was the most beautiful sound I'd ever heard. Cole's hand clenched in mine and I looked over to see raw emotion painted on his beautiful face.

"I didn't know how to tell you," I choked out. "It was my fault, the medication the hospital gave me interfered with my pills," I babbled.

"Shhh, darlin', let me hear our baby," he whispered, his ear turned to the sound.

We sat and listened to the rhythmic sound for a few moments before the nurse pulled the receptors off my belly. "Everything sounds great," she said as she smiled reassuringly. "Baby looks great."

"Good," I sighed, relieved.

"She fainted though," Cole interjected. He was clearly worried and not just about me.

"The doctor on staff can speak to you about that, but the baby sounds fine," she assured us. "I'll just get this out of your way and Dr. Epstein will be in shortly."

I watched her from my place on the exam table as she wheeled the ultrasound equipment out of the room. It felt deathly quiet once she was gone.

"Why didn't you tell me?" Cole asked quietly.

I cringed. "I'm sorry, I didn't know how and I was afraid that you'd feel trapped or something…" I trailed off.

"How long have you known?"

"About a week," I admitted while looking up at the ceiling. We were in one of the urgent care rooms, with a curtain separating the beds. Luckily no one occupied the next bed, but the room felt huge and off-putting, especially given all that had happened that night.

"I just feel so overwhelmed," I admitted, my voice choked as my eyes flooded. "My life has completely turned upside down in the past three months," I said, the tears breaking free and sliding down my face. "Before you I had everything so controlled. I had a grasp on every feeling, every step I made. Then I met you and my world just exploded with emotion and people and life," I breathed. "And I don't know how to trust the happiness and safety that I feel with you, I've never had anything like it. Anything close has been ripped away," I said hoarsely. I felt Cole's hand clench in mine and felt the confidence to continue. "I almost expected something to happen like this, it was too good to be true that I could just move on without retribution," I lamented. "But tonight was something different," I whispered. "I have this life I'm responsible for," I said reverently, my hand grazing my belly. "I've never felt such a ferocity in my life," I told him. "It was like I would stop at nothing to protect this baby. And I know it's so soon and I know we didn't discuss it, but I want this,

Cole," I told him, turning with tear-filled eyes to face him. "But the last thing I want is for you to feel trapped. I only want you to be with me, be with us, if it's what you really want, too," I whispered.

He stared down at me with an unfathomable expression. "Baby, where else would I ever want to be? It is fast, everything about us has been. It's only fitting that you'd get knocked up quickly, too," he said as he chuckled.

"Right," I muttered, not amused as the doctor strode into the room reviewing my chart.

"Well, I see congratulations are in order," he said with a kind smile, wheeling over on a small stool to my bedside. "What brings you here to us this evening?"

"She fainted," Cole answered for me. It didn't need to be said that we'd be leaving the other details of the evening out.

"Oh?" the doctor cocked his head to the side. "Well that can certainly happen during pregnancy, blood flow gets to the brain a bit slower. You need to be careful when you stand up suddenly. Another cause can be anxiety or high stress. I see here that your blood pressure is slightly elevated. Have you been under undue stress?" he asked. His question was almost comical, but Cole's expression confirmed that he found the situation anything but funny.

"A bit," I allowed vaguely.

"Well my advice would be to do whatever you can to remove or reduce that stress for the health of you and your baby," he advised.

"Okay," I answered, though I didn't really see how I had any control over Jake and his insanity.

"Any other questions?"

I looked at Cole, who shook his head. "No I think we're

good, thank you."

"Sure thing. Take care and congratulations again," he said as he smiled.

He left us to it and I rose from the bed to get dressed more than eager to get the hell out of the hospital.

Cole was quiet as we drove home, and though I was concerned about what was going on in his head, I was too tired to give it much thought. I worked a full shift, was attacked, and spent the remainder of the night in the ER. That was about the extent of what I could deal with at the moment. I even went so far as to fall asleep on the drive home, even though it was a short distance from our house.

I woke up when Cole lifted me and carried me inside. I heard Chief's claws clack on the hardwood as he followed us through the dark house. I didn't want to open my eyes to see the overturned furniture or any other proof of my earlier ordeal. Instead, I wanted to slide into oblivion – which is exactly what I did when Cole placed me into bed.

When I woke up, sunlight was streaming through the blinds and I discovered it was after 11 AM when I looked at the clock. Well, it had been a very late night. I could hear Cole's deep voice and I realized that was probably what had woken me. He sounded pissed and I couldn't resist the urge to open our door to try to eavesdrop a bit.

"Endangering not only my woman but also my fucking child!" he was saying. "Whatever we've been doing needs to be stepped up tenfold, and that needed to happen yesterday," he ordered.

Well, I guess we were telling people we're expecting. I rolled my eyes a bit at that.

"I hear you, son," Cal's deep voice replied. "How is she?"

"I don't know, freaked probably," Cole answered sharply. "A maniac broke into our house where she thought she was safe, attacked her, and threatened her. She was scared about the baby," Cole's voice broke a bit with emotion and my heart lurched for him. "But she handled herself well, like she always does." And I could hear the pride in his voice.

"How are you, Bud?" Cal asked, his tone gentle. I felt bad for eavesdropping, but I couldn't seem to stop myself.

"I'm thrilled as hell I knocked her up," he said as he chuckled. "I think she's freaked about that, too, worried about how I really feel about it, probably getting used to the idea herself, but we'll be fine." He sighed, sounding tired. He had to be, it'd been a long night for him, too.

I moved back into the bedroom and curled up on the bed to give them the privacy I should have granted them all along. It wasn't long before I heard the front door close and a Harley roar to life out front.

Cole peeked his head in the room and smiled when he saw I was awake. He was just in his boxers and my eyes traveled his body hungrily. "Come lay down with me," I requested quietly.

He strode into the room with Chief at his heels. "You and Chief friends again?" I asked with an amused smile.

"It would appear so," he nodded while climbing up onto the bed and pulling me into his reassuring warmth.

"How are you?" he asked quietly, his fingers moving through my hair.

I shrugged. "Okay I guess, though I don't feel like anything has really set in yet. I kind of feel like I'm living someone else's life at the moment or something," I tried to explain.

"There's a lot that needs to sink in," he agreed quietly as his fingers traced over my belly. He'd done that several times since he'd learned the news, and I found the gesture to be incredibly sweet and comforting.

"What if we went away for a few days?" I asked, shifting my body to meet his eyes. "Just you and me."

His brows rose at the suggestion before he turned contemplative. "We could do that, it's a great idea actually. Any particular place you want to go?"

"Surprise me," I invited.

"I know just the place," he replied, nuzzling in my neck.

Cole and I spent the whole day together, wanting to be close, whether we were watching TV on the sofa or reading side by side. I wasn't sure if it was the incident with Jake or the pregnancy, but either way, I welcomed the contact. I felt more connected to Cole than ever.

We were seated side by side on the couch as he worked on his laptop and I watched some guilty pleasure reality TV. "What are you looking at?" I asked and laughed when I looked over and noticed a picture of a baby on his laptop screen.

"Just doing some research," he said with a bashful grin.

"Oh?" I quirked my brow at him.

"Yeah, did you know right now the baby is the size of a blueberry?" he asked seriously.

"I didn't know that," I answered, trying to keep a straight face. The sight of my formidable biker pouring over pregnancy websites was beyond adorable.

"You need to be taking folic acid. Are you?" he asked.

"Yeah, babe," I assured him. "I did some research of my own and talked to the doctor when I first went in. I've got it covered," I assured him as I patted his thigh.

"I want to go to every appointment from here on in," he told me sternly. He clearly wasn't happy that he missed the first one.

"Deal," I agreed softly as he wrapped an arm around me and hauled me into his body to look at some pictures of what our blueberry might look like.

Later that evening I was just finishing up getting ready in the bedroom. It had taken some convincing, but I'd been firm with Cole that I still intended to go to the barbecue. As much as I enjoyed our cocoon, I wanted to see everyone.

"Babe, we gotta roll!" Cole's voice hollered from the living room

"Two minutes!" I hollered back. Really, I meant at least five if not ten, but he didn't need to know that.

I couldn't explain exactly why, but looking my best mattered a lot to me tonight. Perhaps it gave me a sense of control, maybe I wanted to assure Benny and Henry that I was okay. Whatever the reason, I was obsessing about my outfit despite it needing to be simple for a casual barbecue. I finally decided on my jean shorts that showed off my toned legs, paired with a kick ass brown belt. I threw on my white V-neck blouse that flattered my chest, and I left my long, red hair down and wild, the way Cole liked it. I completed the look with cowboy boots and light makeup.

Cole let out a low whistle when I finally appeared in the living room.

I blushed.

"Ready?" he asked, pulling me into an embrace and kissing me soundly.

"Ready."

We took the truck so that Chief could come with us, and we had about a cow's worth of ribs to bring. I bought all the ingredients earlier in the day and they'd been marinating to what I hoped was perfection for hours.

Chief had become a regular at the clubhouse and all the guys loved him, now even more so after learning what he'd done for me. He loved being around everyone and I wouldn't dream of leaving him at home.

"Babe, let's not tell everyone about the baby, okay?" I asked after we hit the road.

"Why not?" he asked, clearly disappointed. If I knew my man, he would hire a blimp to scream the news across the sky if he could.

"Because it's really early," I replied turning to face him. "We should wait until we're out of the first trimester. And with everything that's going on, I just want to keep this between us for now," I explained.

"I already told my pop," he admitted, telling me something I already knew.

"That's okay, obviously Kat already knows, too. I don't mind if Sal and Wes know either since they're so close to us, but that's it, okay?"

He put his hand on my thigh intertwining our fingers and squeezed lightly. "Okay, darlin'," he agreed.

A few hours into the evening, I was feeling content lounging on a folding chair by the fire pit with Connie. I kept a plastic cup filled with water in my hand so no one would suspect why I wasn't drinking. Chief lay contentedly at my feet. My ribs had been consumed with vigor, and though I was glad they were so well received, I feared that I was now on the hook to provide them at every get-together.

Despite the recent drama, all the guys seemed ready to

relax and have a good time. The vibe was a positive one and I soaked it in.

"Where's Kat?" Connie asked as she plopped down next to me.

"She'll be here later, Sal is picking her up from work," I replied.

"How are things between those two?" she asked.

I shrugged not wanting to divulge much. Not much had changed as far as I could tell. Kat loved him, but she still felt like she wasn't getting what she needed from him. I wasn't sure what would hurdle them in one direction or the other, but something was going to have to give.

"Rosie, can we talk for a few?" Henry's deep voice rumbled through the night air as he and Benny stood as a formidable pair over us. We'd already exchanged pleasantries, but I knew there would be more of a talk to come.

"I'll go find Wes," Connie excused herself with a "good luck" smile toward me.

"Having fun darlin'?" Henry asked.

"Yeah," I said with a smile as they both sat across from me. Benny had greeted me warmly despite us not having known each other well when my father was alive. He was in his mid-50s with a shaved head and a goatee. He was on the shorter side but no less menacing than Henry when he wanted to be.

"How you holdin' up?" Henry asked, concern darkening his gray eyes.

I shrugged. "Doing the best I can." I didn't know what else to say about it.

"We're doing everything we can to find that fucker. He's a slippery little weasel," Benny grumbled.

"I know you are," I assured him.

"Rosie," Henry started, "now that those fucks are long gone from the club you could come home you know," he offered, surprising me. That was the last thing I'd been expecting. "I know you left because of them. I don't know all the details, but what I do know makes me want to kill him even more now," he added. I didn't doubt that was true. "But they're gone," he said quietly. "You always loved the club and we all love you. I just want you to know there's always a place for you with us even though your daddy's gone," he said sincerely.

"I appreciate that, guys. But my place is with Cole now," I said softly as both men's eyes lifted to look up over my head and I felt a firm grip on my shoulder.

I looked up to meet Cole's warm blue eyes. "Trying to steal my girl fellas?" Cole asked in a light tone, though there was an undertone of threat to it.

"Nah, man. Just want her to know she can always come home," Henry explained.

"She is home," Cole replied without hesitation.

I looked up at him with a slow smile as we exchanged a knowing look. Not only was I home, but we were building a family. In that moment, any trepidation I'd had about the pregnancy evaporated under his reverent stare. I knew I could do this. I could do anything as long as we were together.

"Yeah, I am home," I agreed, beaming.

Chapter Seventeen

We took off for our getaway after breakfast the next day. Cole had shared that his family owned a small cabin near the Nevada-California border in the mountains. It sounded private and beautiful, just what I wanted.

Pete had yet again given me time off. I was probably close to losing my job, but I couldn't bring myself to care with everything else that was going on. Chief seemed to sense that we were embarking on some sort of adventure and happily panted his way through the drive. We both would have loved to take the bike, but we had the dog and too much stuff. I might have slightly over packed. But Cole had just chuckled as he hauled my huge suitcase into the back of the truck.

It was a beautiful fall day and I hoped it would be warm enough to lay out in the sunshine. I smiled blissfully as we headed up into the mountains, Cole's hand on my thigh.

It took us just over two hours to get into town, where we stopped at a local grocery store to load up on supplies before we headed to the cabin.

It was late afternoon as the truck left the paved road and began to kick up gravel as we headed down the private lane to the cabin on the outskirts of town. My curiosity peaked as we traveled down the pine-filled lane and stopped at a rustic looking cabin. The scenery was breathtaking with its lush pine surroundings and turquoise blue water beyond. I was shocked that the cabin was on the lake. I hadn't expected that.

We grabbed our groceries as Chief bounded off into the wilderness to explore. Cole unlocked the door, which opened into the living room. It was a cozy space with hardwood floors and pale blue painted walls. The sliding glass door directly in front of us led to the lake and what looked like its own private pier.

"Wow, this place is amazing," I breathed. The cabin was small but obviously well maintained. And having private access to the lake was unusual.

Cole shrugged. "It needs a lot of updating, but the scenery makes up for it. I haven't been here in years," he told me as we walked through to the white tiled kitchen. I put the bag I held on the counter and looked around. The appliances were old, but looked to be in decent condition. The whole place smelled a bit musty and I started opening the windows to let the fresh air in. There were two bedrooms off the living room, one a bit larger than the other, and Cole put our suitcases in there. The bedrooms had a thick blue rug that made me smile.

"Like I said, needs a bit of updating," he said as he chuckled.

"It's charming." I grinned sincerely, placed my arms around his waist, and kissed his neck.

"It was my ma's family's place," he added while looking down at me.

"Oh?" I asked with a raised brow. He'd never talked

about that side of his family and I was curious.

"Yeah. My grandma left it to my pop in her will," he explained, letting me go but taking my hand as he led me out to the back patio.

"Was she close to your dad?" I asked, leaning on the rail next to him as we looked out to the gorgeous blue water.

"Yeah, I was little when she died. But she spent a lot of time with me. I remember bits and pieces… wish I remembered more," he said with regret. "And she stayed close with my pop when Mom left us."

"Do you ever wonder about her?" I asked, referring to his mother. I'd always wanted to ask him this question since I'd learned that she'd walked out.

He sighed and looked thoughtfully out at the landscape. "I'd be lying if I said I never thought about it. Of course I have. But I try not to spend too much energy on it. She left us," he said casually, though I could sense an undercurrent of pain in his words. "Her loss."

"Absolutely," I agreed readily. "Thanks for bringing me here," I said quietly, sensing he didn't want to talk about it further. "It's beautiful. I'd never expected it to be so private."

He put his arm around my shoulders and pulled me into his side. "It was a good idea to get away for a few days."

"Yeah," I sighed.

The next few days were utter bliss. We slept in late every morning and had coffee out on the patio, watching the water. We'd wander down to the lake and I even got a few chances to don my bikini, though it was too cold to swim. Cole seemed to appreciate the view, judging from how he pounced on me the first time he saw the skimpy red suit. I figured I better wear it while I still could.

In the evenings I cooked, and we again sat on the patio bundled in sweatshirts against the fall chill. We made love every chance we got, which was a lot. And we talked. We talked about our childhoods and about our families. We talked about our friends, both past and present. And we talked about the baby.

"I think it's a boy," Cole asserted confidently as we sat out on the patio watching the sun go down.

I laughed. "There's no way you can know that!"

He shrugged. "It's a hunch."

"Well, then I think it's a girl," I replied just to be contrary.

He groaned. "Christ, the last thing I need is a little girl, especially if she looks like you. I already have my hands full," he grumbled.

"You'll be a wonderful father," I said seriously, ignoring his teasing. I knew he'd be happy with either sex.

"And you'll be a wonderful mother," he said, wrapping an arm around my shoulder.

"I hope so," I whispered, feeling a small knot begin to grow in my throat. "I wish my mom was still here to show me the ropes. I have no idea what I'm doing," I admitted thickly.

He squeezed me close and kissed my head. "We'll figure it out together, darlin', just like we do everything else."

That made me feel better and I nodded.

"I think we'll need a bigger place," he noted, surprising me. The thought hadn't even crossed my mind.

"Really?"

He nodded. "More bedrooms, bigger backyard."

My brows knitted with confusion. "But we have two

bedrooms already."

He squeezed me firmly. "I grew up an only child, babe. We're having at least two."

"At least?" I gulped. I was just now getting used to having one. "Why don't we see how this one works out before we start planning on a fleet," I quipped.

"At least two." He grinned, kissing me.

"We'll see," I grumbled.

"Gonna put a ring on your finger, baby," he added seriously. "You won't know when or where, but just know it's happening."

I stiffened in his arms and pulled back to look at him. "Just because we're having a baby together doesn't mean that we have to get married," I replied, watching as his blue eyes narrowed. I rushed to continue, wanting to get this out. "I just don't want you to feel like you have to… propose," I explained as my eyes scanned the horizon, unable to face him. "We could just see how it goes for a while…." my voice drifted. This had been my biggest fear, that he'd feel forced to marry me. It was the last thing I wanted.

"You're afraid I feel obligated," he surmised correctly.

"Yes," I answered simply.

"Already have the ring, babe," he replied quietly, putting his finger underneath my chin to turn my face to his. "And I've had it for a while," he admitted.

I let out a small laugh in surprise. "Really?"

"Really," he replied seriously as he stared intently into my eyes.

"You're crazy," I teased him, though I was beyond relieved at this news even if it meant he was moving a million miles per hour as usual. I was tempted to ask just how long he'd had it, but I decided against it.

"Maybe so, but you're stuck with me," he said with a grin, his mood lightening.

"Yeah, I am." I grinned back, leaning in to kiss him.

I felt far from ready when we packed up and headed home. After three full days of nothing but Cole and relaxation, I wanted nothing to do with going home. But duty called for both of us and I reluctantly piled into the truck with Chief.

"Ready?" Cole said as he grinned and started up the truck.

"No," I grumbled.

He reached over and gave my leg a reassuring squeeze. "We'll come back, darlin'," he promised when he sensed my disappointment.

"Good," I replied with a small smile.

Chapter Eighteen

We'd been home for two weeks from the cabin and so far all had been quiet. Sal had painstakingly replaced the security system in our house, adding even more bells and whistles. He'd been beyond pissed that Jake had breached his original system. The thing seemed impenetrable now, which was both reassuring and annoying. I felt like I lived at the CIA headquarters with all the different motion detectors and codes I had to remember. Cole had stepped up all security when it came to me, but I accepted it without complaint, knowing it was needed and that he worried.

I was still feeling pretty good as my pregnancy progressed. I'd heard all kinds of horror stories of morning sickness, headaches, and food aversions. So far, aside from feeling more tired than normal and having tender breasts, I still felt like me.

As promised, we took dinner over to Cal's place and had a really special evening looking through pictures of him and my father. There were several of Cole and me playing together as young kids. I marveled again at what a small world it seemed to be.

"If that ain't destiny, I don't know what is," Cal said

as he chuckled, his eyes twinkling with delight. Cole had looked at me with such warmth and love that I had to choke back tears. I never thought much about destiny, but I suppose I believed in it when it came to Cole and me.

We rode home that night through the cool night air and I felt a peace I'd never felt in my life. It had been growing in me since I met Cole. It persisted despite everything that had happened, and I marveled at its ability to grow regardless of the drama that surrounded us. I clutched Cole's strong body in my arms as the bike rumbled beneath me. I felt beyond lucky.

I should have realized that my luck would run out.

"Babe, I gotta go," Cole's voice woke me through the darkness of our bedroom.

"Hmm, what time is it?" I murmured.

"Just after two. I'm getting called out. Knox is on his way to watch the house. I'll be back as soon as I can," he told me, kissing my head as I drifted back to sleep.

When Cole wasn't back the next morning, I felt a frisson of worry, but I tried to brush it off. I assumed whatever he had to do had just taken longer than expected. But when my phone started ringing with an unknown number, my breakfast immediately solidified in my gut. I just knew something was terribly wrong.

"Scarlet, baby, how are you?" Jake's voice came through the phone.

"What did you do?" I hissed.

"Nothing that wasn't necessary," he said casually and my blood ran cold. "You want him in one piece, you're going to have to come get him, alone," he growled.

"How do I know he's okay?" I rasped as panic seized me.

"You're just going to have to trust me."

"Trust you?" I choked incredulously.

"It's your only option. I'm at our old hideout. I thought it was appropriate," he said and chuckled darkly. "You tell anyone, he's dead. You try anything sneaky, he's dead. You come alone, and without that beast of yours," he instructed. "Then you and I, we're going to take off. And your precious blondie here can keep his life. I figure it's more of a punishment to lose you to me anyway," he snorted.

There was no way in hell I was going to let that happen.

"I'll be there," I said quietly. I didn't have much choice.

"Can't wait, baby," he replied, and the excitement in his voice made me want to throw up.

I was shocked at how clear-headed I felt when I hung up. It was up to me not only to protect Cole but our unborn child as well. I knew I couldn't risk going alone, as much as I didn't want to risk Cole's safety he'd never forgive me if I did something that put me and our baby in danger. I needed backup, but I had to be smart about it.

I didn't know how clever Jake was being about this, my instinct said not much, but I planned to err on the side of caution. I drove to Jupiter and used the phone behind the bar. I called Cal and on the very off-chance Jake was somehow tracking, I knew I couldn't give him any details over the phone.

"Yeah?" he answered, sounding gruff. He didn't recognize the number.

"Hi Cal, it's Scarlet," I said quickly.

"Oh, hi darlin'." He clearly sounded surprised to hear from me and a bit wary, which I expected. "What's doin'?"

I needed something that would tip him off, I knew he'd

be smart and not press me over the phone.

"Cole's oversleeping like usual. I forgot my wallet and was hoping you could drop it by my work," I asked quietly. We both knew Cole never overslept, in fact, he was an absurdly early riser.

"Sure thing, be there in ten," he answered without delay.

We sat side by side at the bar amidst the hustle and bustle of the lunch hour rush and I looked around trying not to appear as terrified as I felt.

"I wasn't followed," Cal stated confidently.

I blew out a breath and turned to face him. "Jake somehow got a hold of Cole. He's got him up in the old army bunkers off Route 1," I told him, my voice shaking. "He called this morning, told me I needed to come alone. I think he plans to take off with me somewhere," I continued, my voice surprisingly calm.

I watched Cal's entire body stiffen and eyes narrow as he tried visibly to remain calm.

"If it wasn't for the baby, I wouldn't have risked telling you. I would have gone alone, but I knew Cole would be so upset if…."

"You did the right thing," he interrupted me firmly, reaching out to give my arm a reassuring squeeze.

"I think I still have to go in alone. I'm too afraid that he'll shoot Cole on sight if he spots anyone else," I said as my eyes swept the room. "And I think I have a plan if you're up for it," I offered.

Cal looked at me in surprise. "What's the plan?" he asked.

I didn't delay in telling him exactly what I conjured up, and before I knew it I was behind the wheel of my

Pathfinder, off to get my man.

It took me four hours to get to the deserted army base, just a mile outside of my hometown in northern California. It was the longest drive of my life. I knew that Cal, Sal, Wes, and Mack were somewhere behind me, but I never once saw them, which was a good thing, since this whole plan would be shot to shit if they were spotted.

I hadn't been back home in almost nine years, and despite everything, I couldn't help but think of my father, long ago lost but never far from my mind. This was the last place I'd seen him alive. This was where my mother, father, and I had been a family. I'd lost a lot within these city limits.

Jake and I had played here as kids, the old bunkers making perfect forts. It was a typically foggy day in the coastal town, and the weather made the old abandoned buildings appear even more sinister and unwelcoming than I'd remembered. Jake and I had terrorized each other mercilessly, hiding in the dark corners and pouncing on each other. We'd shared countless meals and played endless games of make-believe within the dilapidated walls. That felt like a lifetime ago.

I had one thing going for me, Jake wanted me and I intended to play that to my advantage. He was also alone with no further allies. I knew that my plan was risky given his obviously volatile mental state, but I was sure it was the best bet we had.

My whole body pumped with adrenaline when I pulled up to the bunker we'd played in most frequently. I cut the engine and sat for a few moments with the pounding of my heart roaring in my ears. Cole had saved me in more ways than one. Yes, he'd kept me safe, but he also saved me from a life of solitude where I hadn't really been living at all. I'd been going through the motions, I'd been surviving, but that was a far cry from what my life is now. Now, he needed me, and I wasn't about to let him down. I steeled myself to what I knew I had to do and I got out of the car.

"That was quick," Jake said as he laughed, making me jump when he emerged from the bunker with a gun in his hand. He strode toward me with purpose and dragged me inside. Despite the dim light, I immediately clocked Cole's slumped form in the corner. He looked lucid as his beautiful eyes met mine and widened in panic. I took a quick perusal of his body and was relieved to see that he didn't look seriously hurt. He had some blood running down the side of his face and his arm but he was alive. Thank God, he was alive. He was gagged, and it took everything I had not to run over to him to assure him I could take care of him, of us. It was the hardest thing I'd ever done, to keep my face clear of emotion as I looked him over. I couldn't give myself away, not if this was going to work.

"Yeah, well, I've been waiting," I replied softly, turning my attention back to Jake with what I hoped was an expectant expression.

It was time for an Oscar-worthy performance.

I saw his brows knit momentarily in confusion.

I sighed as though exasperated. "He's had me followed, the house under surveillance," I explained. "I was ready to come to you on my own, I just didn't know how."

Jake's eyes narrowed and he backhanded me across the face. "Don't you dare fuck with me! What, do you think I'm fucking stupid?" he growled as I saw Cole struggling to get up. I knew it was killing him to be so helpless. But I had this handled, or I hoped I did. I held my hand to my cheek and blinked a few times while the initial sting subsided.

"Do you want to hear me out or do you want to hit me some more?" I demanded angrily.

I was so tired of him knocking me around.

He regarded me intently for a few excruciatingly long moments before he made a motion for me to continue. "I had to get away for a while, Jake," I explained, hoping my tone was placating enough. "After my dad died, I didn't know where my place was, and I felt confused. By the time I decided to come home, come back to you, I'd already gotten all tangled up with the Knights," I explained trying to look ashamed and a bit disgusted. "And then Henry and Benny were back in the picture – and there wasn't a way that I could see to get out of it," I pleaded with him to understand as he looked at me with a guarded expression. "That night that you came for me, I wanted so badly for you to understand, but he has the house bugged and I couldn't tell you…." I drifted off as he seemed to hang onto my every word. "I couldn't tell you that I know I need to be with you. I've loved you since I was a little girl," I said, nearly choking with disgust at the lie. "If you still want me, let's just go. Leave him here," I gestured toward Cole with what I hoped looked to be utter dispassion. "It can be just you and me, like it used to be." I smiled tentatively at him, hoping against hope that he was buying this. I hated that Cole had to witness it.

I just needed long enough for him to let his guard down, and though he was skeptical, I could tell that he wanted badly to believe me. All I wanted was to keep Cole alive. If we got through this, Cole was going to be seriously pissed with me.

"So you wouldn't care if I killed him then?" Jake

taunted, taking a few steps closer to Cole and playing with his gun. Luckily I'd known he'd test me with this and I was prepared.

"Yes, I care," I scoffed. "If you kill him, the Knights will never stop coming after us. Is that what you want? Let's be smart about this Jake," I implored. "Let's just go. I even packed my stuff before I left," I said hopefully.

"You did?" he asked with raised brows. For some reason that fact seemed to convince him more than anything I'd said.

It was a lie, but I was going with it.

"Yes. I've had a bag packed for weeks. I just needed an opportunity," I said as I grinned and grabbed his arm. "Come on, I'm afraid I was followed. Let's get the hell out of here," I said insistently.

He pulled me close and the feel of his body against mine was so repulsive that I nearly shook with disgust. This man had assaulted me, stalked me, and killed my father. But I would do anything to keep Cole safe. He looked down at me with raw emotion and I knew I had him. "Ah, babe I've waited so long for you to come around. I knew you would," he said as he grinned. He leaned over and kissed me. I'd been prepared for this, too, but it was still even more unpleasant than I'd bargained for. Everything about his mouth on mine was repugnant, and I had to fight the urge not to shove him off. Instead, I put my arms around him and pulled him closer. I could hear Cole's grunts of anger, but I couldn't risk giving him any sort of sign to cool it.

"Ready?" I asked, breaking away as soon as I felt I'd made a believable enough impression.

"Yeah, I just really gotta give this bastard one more

kick," he said with a smirk. He put the gun he'd been holding in the waistband of his jeans and I knew this was my chance. I pulled the gun out of the back of my jeans and held it to the side of his head before he could move any closer to Cole. I couldn't believe it, my hands weren't even shaking.

"Not one step closer," I said sharply. I saw Jake's entire body freeze and I held my ground, bracing for whatever was in store. I couldn't even look at Cole for fear of the look on his face.

"You fucking cunt!" he roared, turning the full extent of his rage toward me. He looked completely demented as he took a menacing step toward me.

"Not another step. I swear to God Jake, I will fucking shoot you," I said sharply. Adrenaline raced through my veins as I held the gun facing him, my feet planted firmly on the ground. "Give me your gun," I commanded.

He snorted. "You're going to have to come get it," he leered, raising the front of his shirt so I could see the gun that was shoved down his pants.

I wrinkled my nose in disgust.

"So what's the plan now, baby?" he taunted.

My plan was to have the guys come bursting in at any moment, but for now it looked like I was on my own.

Understanding showed on his face and he smirked. "Got friends comin', huh? Well, if you think for one second I'm going to stand here and wait, then you are out of your fucking mind," he hissed.

"And if you think I'm going to let you walk out of here only to let you continue to fuck up my life, then you're out of yours," I retorted. "Don't fucking move." I was shocked at how calm and collected I felt. I was beyond done letting this psycho fuck with me.

"Not gonna let me walk out, huh? Well, if I'm staying, I won't be breathing soon, no confusion about that. So if I'm going, I'm taking you with me. He can come, too," he said, gesturing to Cole with a manic glint in his eye.

Shit, I was going to have to shoot him. I really, really didn't want to do that. It wasn't that I cared about Jake's well-being. He'd done enough to me to ensure that. But I still didn't want to be responsible for taking someone's life.

"Jake," my voice was practically a whisper. "If any part of you still cares about me – if you ever cared about me at all, then please do not make me do this," I pleaded. It was the first time I'd shown any real emotion since I'd walked into this mess.

"Don't you get it, Scarlet? I care about you more than anything. That's why I can't let you go. If I'm going, you're coming, too," he replied, his own voice hoarse with emotion.

The resulting shot that rang out lit up the dark bunker with blinding light and a thunderous sound.

Chapter Nineteen

"Baby, wake up, we're home," Cole's deep voice murmured as I felt a warm hand brush against my cheek.

I woke up groggily for a moment before remembering that I was in the back of Wes's SUV. It was very early morning with a hint of dawn in the air as I stepped out in front of our house. I looked over at Cole, relieved to see him standing whole and strong in front of me.

A large amount of the blood I'd seen on him had been from the initial head wound he sustained when Jake took him by surprise with a tire iron. During the drive, I'd gotten the story that the guys had indeed called Cole out for a club errand. Jake must have been following him because he jumped him at a gas station and sedated him with something.

We'd stopped at a hospital on our way back to get Cole stitched up. I couldn't believe he was lucky enough to only need ten stitches to sew up the gash. I was still reeling from everything that had transpired, and I stood on wobbly legs trying to pull myself together. I knew I'd done well during the ordeal, but now that it was over I was on the verge of a meltdown. I'd almost lost Cole, I'd almost been killed.

Cal, Wes, and Sal had arrived just in time, and Cal shot Jake once in the chest. I didn't think I'd ever get Jake's expression out of my head. It was as though he was shocked that it was over, that he'd lost. He looked more pissed off than anything. But I watched him die, and it would take a while to recover from that, if I ever did at all.

"Cole, man," I heard Wes warn as my knees started to give out. I was swept up in Cole's arms before I had the chance to fall and he carried me into the house.

"I've got you, baby," he said softly in my ear.

I laid my head on his shoulder, wrapping my arms more firmly around his neck, trying to get as close to him as possible. Chief was all over us as soon as he opened the door, but Cole commanded him softly to be still. I was vaguely aware of Cole carrying me into our bathroom, of my bloody clothes being peeled off. He got me into the shower and tenderly cleaned my body and hair. I just closed my eyes and let him care for me. I knew he must be tired, he'd been through the same ordeal as me and he was injured. But he needed to do this and I needed to let him.

When we finally got into bed, the sun was out and a new day was beginning. Cole pulled me into his body and stroked my bare back. He hadn't bothered with clothes for either one of us. The skin to skin contact was just what I needed. I fell asleep almost immediately, relishing in the comfort of his hold on me.

When I woke up, I realized I had barely moved. I was still lying on Cole, my legs entangled with his. I looked at the clock to find that it was nearly dinnertime. We'd slept all day.

I looked up and found Cole's blue eyes staring into mine. "Hey," I said, my voice raspy.

"Hi," he said as he smiled tenderly, leaning down to kiss me.

"How do you feel?" I asked as I eyed the bandage on the side of his head.

"Okay, bit of a headache," he replied. "How do you feel?" his eyes were full of concern.

"I'm okay, we're okay," I amended, swallowing audibly. I paused for a beat before I could continue. "It will take me a long time to recover from what I saw, but I knew it needed to happen in order to save us. I just... you know his expression," I drifted off as the lump in my throat got bigger.

"I know," he murmured, squeezing me.

"But I'm here and you're here. I'd give anything for that. I'd go through anything for you," I said quietly while staring up at him.

He looked down at me with an unfathomable expression before he reached over me and grabbed something out of his nightstand.

"I had a much more romantic proposal in mind," he said. My eyes widened in surprise as he opened a ring box to reveal an exquisite diamond ring. "But life is short. I don't want to wait any longer to put this on your finger," he told me, his voice gruff with emotion. "I want you to be my wife, I want us to make the family that neither of us had," he said, slipping the ring onto my finger.

"I want that, too," I whispered, staring up at him with a love so huge it felt like my heart would burst from it.

"Marry me," he murmured, his lips against mine.

"Yes," I whispered back, smiling against his mouth as I wrapped my arms around his shoulders. True, it may not have been the most romantic or outlandish proposal, but

I couldn't have pictured it any other way – just Cole and me in our bed.

I snuck a peak at the ring and gasped, pleasantly surprised. It was a gorgeous oval diamond with an antique setting. It was timeless and classic, and I loved it.

"Like it?" his voice rumbled against my neck.

"It's perfect," I beamed.

"Good, how about you show me some appreciation?" he asked, his mouth trailing down from my neck to my nipple.

"I think that sounds like a plan," I agreed.

Epilogue

A month later...

I ran out to meet Cole at the curb where he sat on his bike in front of Jupiter. He'd come to pick me up from my last day of work.

My mentality about things had changed since the last and final incident with Jake. Life was short and I was determined to make the most of every moment. That included quitting a job that I'd been phoning in for years. I was going back to school for nursing. I wanted to do something bigger with my life. I wanted to do something I could be proud of, that my family could be proud of.

I was in my second trimester now and my body had started to visibly change. I had slightly bigger breasts and a small bump that grew day by day. Cole assured me every day that I looked more beautiful than ever as I fretted over getting fat.

"You're not going to get fat, babe," he'd always tell me. "You're pregnant and you look fucking sexy as hell."

I believed him since he proved on a daily basis that he thought so. I could barely keep him off me long enough to get anything done.

I accepted the helmet from his outreached hand and kissed him before hopping up behind him. We roared off, and I felt the same rush I always did when I was with him on the bike.

The last month had been a time for recovery. I'd had nightmares for the first couple of weeks after Jake had been killed. Cole had woken with me each and every time and held me until I settled back in. His unconditional support and unyielding patience were largely how I'd made it to the other side. The guys had all been amazing, too. Despite Cole's aggravation at me for pulling my stunt with Jake, the guys all seemed to think it was pretty badass. I'd always had their respect, but now I seemed to have it tenfold.

Cal in particular had become more of a presence. He and I continued to forge a bond that had been born from a love of my father, and it continued through our mutual love of his son. Cole and I had dinner with him at least once a week, and I watched as their bond of father and son grew stronger.

Aside from my own healing, the last month had been spent healing Kat's wounds as well. Sal had taken off a week after Jake died. He told her he needed some space and had been vague about where he was going or if he'd be coming back. She was understandably devastated. Cole seemed as baffled as the rest of us, but was confident that Sal would "get his shit straight" as he put it. Kat was determined not to wait around. She felt like he'd jerked her around enough already. But he was her first love and it would take time.

She stayed with us for the first few days, but had quickly moved into the studio apartment that Cole and I had helped her find. The old place had too many memories, she needed a fresh start. I was concerned with how quickly she seemed to want to move past it all. She needed time to grieve, but I just tried to support her as best I could. She still hung around with the guys sometimes, but it seemed to remind her too much of Sal for the time being. She and I largely did our own thing when I wasn't with Cole. Day by day it seemed to get easier for her.

For my part, I finally felt like all my demons had been laid to rest. Jake and everything that came with him was dead and gone. Cole and I were building a life together, a life I was living every second of. My past was no longer baggage I had to bear the weight of, it was simply that, my past. I could bring my parents back into the light and not bury them deep in a place that no one could touch. Instead, they were all around us. They were in the photos that Cal had given us that we'd since hung up in our home. They were in the stories Cal told. They'd be in our child's smile.

My father had met a violent end, but I knew with certainty that he had peace now that I had Cole – a man who cared for me above all else, what else could a father want for his daughter?

The bike rumbled down our street and I grinned as our house came into view. I'd been able to convince Cole to stay in it for now. I'd had enough upheaval and I just wanted to settle. For now we had more than enough room, we could always expand later.

Chief greeted us enthusiastically as he always did when we walked in the door. He had quickly become an irreplaceable part of our family, I couldn't imagine life without him.

I looked around our welcoming home and sighed in contentment.

"Happy, baby?" Cole asked, coming to stand behind me and as he so often did and he placed his hands on my belly.

"Yeah, honey, more than I ever imagined I'd be." I smiled, turning my face to look into his gorgeous blue eyes.

"It's just the beginning, you know," he said with a grin.

He was right, our story was just beginning and I promised myself I'd enjoy every second of the ride.

The End

Thank you for reading!

The Ride Series continues with the story of Sal and Kat. Available now!

To find more information on the Ride Series, Megan O'Brien's other titles, and ways to follow and connect with Megan, please visit:

meganobrienbooks.com

Megan O'Brien is the best selling author of the Ride Series and the Talon Security Series. She has a passion for a good love story and most enjoys writing stories with an alpha male and strong female characters.

Megan was born and raised in Marin County, California where she still resides with her amazing husband and three lovely children.

When she's not enjoying family time or burying her nose in her kindle she loves hiking, running and relaxing moments on the back porch with a glass of wine.

Fall in love with all the men of the Knights MC in the Ride Series!

Follow the men of Talon Security as the ex military security specialists work together to protect the women they love and each other in this contemporary romance series.

Made in United States
North Haven, CT
31 March 2022

17751401R00134